Romantic Times: Vegas

I0553533

Tina Wainscott

Crystal Perkins

Amanda McIntyre

Hailey J. Bissell

Tina DeSalvo

Sabrina York

Carole Nelson Douglas

Kathryn Falk, Lady of Barrow

13Thirty Books
Print and Digital Editions
Copyright 2016

Discover new and exciting works by 13Thirty Books at
www.13thirtybooks.com

Print and Digital Edition, License Notes

ISBN: 069266727X
ISBN-13: 978-0692667279

DEDICATION

To all the amazing people at Romantic Times who over the years have changed so many lives in so many positive ways.

CONTENTS

ACKNOWLEDGMENTS

Judy Spagnola
For all her hard work in making this anthology possible

And to
Rick Taubold for his editorial assistance

FOREWORD

Kathryn Falk, Lady of Barrow

Kisses and hugs to 13Thirty Books for compiling a Romance Anthology: *Romantic Times: Vegas*, to entertain the readers at the 33rd RT Booklovers Convention 2016 in Las Vegas.

The lineup of authors is quite varied and impressive, starting with my longtime friend, **Heather Graham**, author of over 150 romances and thrillers. She began writing Romance novels at the same time I started a tabloid publication, *Romantic Times*, now *RT Book Reviews*, and the Booklovers Convention—despite people saying I was crazy to do so.

Several name authors in this collection were also involved in the early days of the Romance genre. It was a much different industry then, smaller and less chaotic. We pushed a lot of envelopes with our stories.

Christina Skye was a Chinese scholar and spoke fluent Mandarin when she appeared on the scene and expressed a desire to write Regencies.

Carole Nelson Douglas, a prominent journalist, stayed in the St. Paul Pioneer Press office till after midnight to help the Romance cause by placing a story of the RT Love Train on the "wires," as it was called in those days. This activated nation-wide coverage for the dozens of authors aboard Amtrak, greeting romance readers (dressed in pink) at stations large and small as we headed from Los Angeles to meet up with Barbara Cartland at the 2nd RT Booklovers Convention in New York City.

Who can forget when contemporary author **Tina Wainscott** arrived at a Convention straight from Russia—having finally succeeded in adopting a baby girl (now 13 years old)—to share her happiness and tins of Russian caviar with her delighted sister authors.

Last but not least, there's no one like our romantic publishers: **Lance Taubold** was one of RT's first cover model contestants, from the Fabio days, as well as being a wonderful singer/entertainer. **Rich Devin** masterfully directed many RT Cover Model Pageants and Awards Ceremonies. It would not be the same biz without them!

RT is fortunate to have loyal friends who are still supporting us after three decades! Ken, Carol, and I are very lucky in this regard and so appreciative.

How romantic it is to come together now *under the covers*, (Sorry for the pun!) and to be writing stories about romantic times in Las Vegas.

Readers will be pleasantly surprised to recognize the names of three prominent authors of Romance who disappeared from the scene for a few years, but have returned to contribute to this collection: Rebecca Paisley, Doris Parmett, and Kimberly Cates.

The three anthologies are rounded out by a talented group of "relatively" new newcomers, including a Barnes & Noble bookseller/author—Crystal Perkins.

A huge thank you to all the authors who brought their imagination and creativity to produce the first RT Convention Anthologies.

To understand how the project developed. Every author received these directives from the publisher:

1) Write a story set in Las Vegas with action taking place inside an imaginary hotel, the Excelsior, built in 1960 by a Mafia family. (That was rather common in those days.)

2) Choose a time frame ranging from 1960 to the present, and even the future, in any genre.

Therefore, dear reader, you will encounter—at the Excelsior Hotel—a vampire, a post-apocalyptic romance, a time-travel suspense, a Fabio-to-the-Rescue comedy and more...

All our Romances have happy endings of course. And the Romance formula even in short fiction will ring true—getting an alpha male to commit!

Enjoy!

Kathryn Falk, Founder of RT Book Reviews and the RT Booklovers Convention

And...

Kenneth Rubin, President of Romantic Times Inc. (He slept his way to the top!)

Carol Stacy, Publisher and Executive Convention Director.

1

CRAZY LOVE

Tina Wainscott

Kate's brother has disappeared, leaving only a cryptic note and the name of the man she gave up so she could care for her bipolar twin. On the last day of the deadline that Sam gave her to let him be part of her crazy life, they must work together to find her twin, who's given them a deadline of his own.

I knew the moment I walked into the apartment that my brother was gone. And I mean *gone*, gone, like on another "deep, dark plunge," his term for it. Maybe it was the twin thing. Maybe I was just bone-wearily experienced at sensing it.

Oscar's room was as cave-like as ever, with foil sealed tightly over the one window. Posters tacked to the walls reflected his bipolar states: *Zoolander* and *Nightmare on Elm Street*. I inched toward the closet, my hand frozen in a claw as I gripped the round handle and pulled.

I breathed out in a gust, half laugh, half sigh of relief. No Oscar hanging there.

He didn't answer my call and text. I ran into the kitchen and checked our DPOC notepad, the "designated place of communication," as he called it. Only one thing was scrawled on it in Oscar's jagged handwriting: my ex-boyfriend's name.

What?

Oscar hated Sam with more passion than I could imagine. Possibly because I loved him with more passion than I could have imagined. Oscar's outbursts increased during the six months we dated, clearly threatened by my feelings for Sam. It was stupid of me, thinking

I could have a life. Love. I could never put my brother in a mental hospital, and I couldn't expect any man to co-exist with him.

With Sam, I had broken my biggest rule—never fall in love. Date, have fun, flirt, but at the hint of a man wanting more, I always came clean about my high-maintenance brother who would likely be my roommate for life. That sent them packing.

I didn't even tell Sam about my brother during the first four months we dated. I was a normal woman of twenty-five, without encumbrances or baggage. I felt carefree, letting myself love the way he pampered me and how he treated me like a lady. An amazing time, other than all the white lies about why he couldn't come to my home, along with my "work" emergencies, piling up around us. I came clean when he began to suspect I was married. No, just harboring a bipolar twin brother. When I cried as it all came out, Sam simply held me. And said we could manage this.

I let myself believe that until... well, until we couldn't manage it. I broke it off. He'd given me three months to change my mind; if I didn't, he planned to reenlist in the Marines. Tomorrow was the deadline.

I grabbed my purse and headed to the Excelsior, where he lived and worked. But I wouldn't be asking him to stay. I'd be asking...

"What the hell happened between you and my brother?" I blurted out the moment Sam opened his hotel room door. I didn't want to give him even a second to think I was there for any other reason.

But I saw it, that flash of happy surprise before I squashed it. I let myself drink him in, with his tousled brown hair that had only recently grown out from the military cut. His blue-gray eyes that now filled with unhappy surprise at my turgid question. His mouth that moved without words as he tried to formulate a response. He wore only jeans, his chest bare and muscular, his skin amber in the soft light. My eyes went to the scar on his chest that I dubbed the shooting star, then back to his face.

"Kate... we should probably talk inside."

I saw clothes stacked up neatly beside an open suitcase by the door. Bed made military style, always before the maid could even come in. He was packing. Going back to that horrible war. Because he said he needed purpose.

I had to focus. Oscar was my forever, not Sam. "I know you spoke to my brother, and now he's missing."

"And you think I've done something to him?"

It had sounded like an accusation, I realized. Though Sam could be a lethal weapon, he'd been incredibly patient with Oscar's outbursts, his accusations of Sam using me, and even more vile scenarios concocted by a manic mind. I reigned in all of the emotions zinging through me like an electric buzz. "No, of course not. But he's gone, and the only clue he left was your name on the DPOC—"

He placed his hands on my shoulders, something he'd done many times when things escalated at my apartment and I felt as though I were catching Oscar's mental illness. "I want you to take a breath, Kate." Sam held my gaze, hypnotizing me to obey. "In... and out."

I did obey, finding my center again; in the feel of his hands on my shoulders and in the steadiness of his eyes. "You always could calm me down," I whispered.

And rev me up. Like no one else.

"There, that's better. I haven't talked to him. Nor has he come here," Sam scrubbed his fingers through his damp hair. "Though I've been in the shower for the last hour."

"*Hour?*"

"Just thinking. Didn't realize how much time had passed until I got out."

I glanced at the luggage. "Getting your mind wrapped around the idea of going back?" I thought my heart couldn't sink any farther, but it did. The thought of his putting himself back in danger, on top of Oscar's situation, pushed me to say, "You could, you know, stay in Vegas. We could... see each other casually."

It felt wrong even as the words came out of my mouth. To him as well, since he was shaking his head. "It's all or nothing with me, Kate. You know that."

"I do, but I was thinking that these last few months being apart would make it easier to—"

"Be friends with benefits?" he cut in, a sharp arch to his eyebrow. Then he completely surprised me by stepping forward and covering my mouth with his, kissing me deep and hard, his hands sliding down my back. Possessively. Knowingly.

I lost myself in him the way I always did, my hands seeking out his waist. I leaned into him, absorbing his strength and comfort and heat.

He broke the kiss softly, moving back enough to look at me. "Think we could really manage that casual thing, Kate?"

I shook my head and limped farther back, before I fell forward again like every cell in my body wanted to. "No. I see that now. It's just that. . ."

"I know," he finished, and I saw that he did. He knew my pain, my angst, my obligations. "I also know that Oscar is your shield against being hurt. Your reason for holding back."

I bristled. "You think I *like* losing you? That I'm happy being alone, without love?"

"No, but I do think you feel safe in your chaotic world. It's comfortable, even if it's difficult."

I wanted to refute his gently spoken words, to throw them back in his face much harder than he'd given them to me. But nothing came out of my mouth. Surely it wasn't true? "I need to find Oscar. I'm sorry I bothered you."

I started to turn, but he grabbed my arm. "Let me help. I know the building. If he left my name on the DORK pad—"

"DPOC," I corrected automatically, our old joke. "Go on."

"He wanted you to come here. Is he working today?"

"No, he's off."

That's how Sam and I met. I'd brought Oscar to work and played a little blackjack. The guy at the next seat had flirted with me, but he'd been drinking and was a little too aggressive. When I left the table, he followed me, still trying to hit me up. I told him to leave me alone, and he started calling me a tease and a snob. A handsome, deadly-calm security guard moved in and escorted him away. I remained in the noisy confines of the Excelsior's casino, giving the guy enough time to leave the premises. And I wanted to thank my savior. Once he got off duty, we spent the rest of the night talking and laughing, watching the sun rise over Vegas.

My text chimed, and I yanked the phone from my purse. "It's him," I said on a breath. I read the text aloud, my voice growing more raw with each word. "My darling sister, I hope you're with Sam. I've explained it all to him. I see now that I've been holding you back. I told myself Sam was the reason you cry at night, because he was an asshole. But I know now that it's because of me.

"A second text. 'As of six o'clock tonight, I will no longer be your responsibility. I'll be fine, and you can finally stop worrying about me. I didn't tell you my plans because I knew you'd try to talk me out of it. Katie, I'm in my right mind, I swear. And I'm happy. I really am.

The meds are working fine. See you on the other side. Love, Oscar."
My heart jammed up as I met Sam's eyes in question.

"He hasn't explained anything to me." Sam glanced over at the nightstand, but the phone's message light wasn't blinking. "He must have come while I was showering."

I called his number, but it rolled to voice mail. "Oscar, please, don't do this! I'm here at the Excelsior. Just tell me where you are. Let's talk."

"Let me grab a shirt and shoes, and we'll go down to the front desk and see if he left a message there."

I wanted to tell him how grateful I was for his assistance... his company and support, if nothing else. But I couldn't push out words. My brother was going to kill himself. *For me.* And he was going to do it here, where he knew every nook and cranny.

Sam had come to the same conclusion, because the moment he pulled on his shirt, he said, "We'll find him before he does anything stupid."

I didn't know how he could promise that, but I ate those words hungrily.

He slid into black boots, grabbed my hand, and tugged me out the door. He didn't let go the entire elevator ride down to the lobby, where the front desk clerk verified that there were no messages, nor was the phone system malfunctioning.

Sam glanced at his high-tech watch. "We have—"

"Three hours and twelve minutes," I said. "To search a hundred-thousand-million square foot casino."

Again, Sam braced his hands on my shoulders, holding my gaze. Then he pulled me close and whispered into my hair, "Don't give up. I learned that in the military, that no matter how bleak, how dire, things look, there is always hope. Even when the woman you love tells you there's no chance for us."

I leaned back, my heart squeezed tight. "You mean you never gave up?" I wanted to hear him say no and I prayed he said yes.

"I stayed the whole three months. And here you are."

"But—"

He silenced me with a quick kiss. "Let's find him."

He had a point. I *was* there, due to Oscar's machinations. But if he took his life in some hare-brained attempt to free me, how could I take that freedom with any kind of peace?

Sam's fingers tight on mine, he headed toward one of the employee elevators away from the shine and lights and gloss. This car had no brass doors or trim, no mirrors or music inside its florescent-lit, scuffed interior.

"Where are we going?" I asked.

"The roof."

Those two words sent my heart plummeting even as we went up. Sam's mouth flattened into a tight line, as though he too was imagining the implications.

"This has happened before?" I asked, afraid for the answer.

He gave her a sharp nod. "The first month I started here, a guest somehow managed to get to the roof. I saw a lot of carnage over in Afghanistan, but the sight of someone who'd thrown their life away, who'd given up... "He shook his head. "Not to mention potential collateral damage. From way up there, you can't always see if there are people below."

"I can't imagine that Oscar would chance it. Even in his lowest times, he's never disregarded others' safety."

"How has he been lately?" he asked, slipping into efficient soldier mode. "Cycling high or low?"

He'd learned some of the vernacular during our attempt to make it work.

"Right after we... broke off, he cycled high for two days, talking incessantly about how I'd narrowly escaped all kinds of scenarios of paranoia that he concocted. When he crashed, I was able to get him to his doctor. He changed Oscar's meds again and ordered him to attend a support group at a church three blocks from my place. It took some tweaking with the new drug, but he's been stable for the last two months. His medication disappears on schedule. The group meets while I'm working, but he swears he's attending and enjoying it. He's even named people he likes, including a woman I think he especially likes."

"So no indication of this at all?"

"None. Unless... he was making it all up." Anything was possible. "One odd thing: I swear he's been snooping in my room. Books have been moved on my shelves, statues shifted. He denies it."

"What about the crying?"

I shook my head. "I haven't heard him cry at all lately."

Sam touched my chin, lifting it so that my eyes met his. "I mean you crying."

I was saved from answering when the elevator doors opened. He reluctantly released me and led me off. We navigated a narrow hallway and even narrower metal stairs before reaching a door. He searched a ring of keys for the right one, and a few seconds later we stepped out into the blinding sun.

My eyes scanned the vast network of towers and equipment that could easily hide a man crouching on the edge, seeking out the best place to land.

Sam slipped back into soldier mode, methodically searching, turning corners, walking quietly and gesturing for me to follow in the same manner. Of course, we wouldn't want to startle Oscar into falling. Maybe he'd be waiting, hoping for a last-minute reprieve.

But I doubted that. He'd sounded so certain about what he was doing. And he thought he was freeing me. *Dumb bastard!*

Dumb, sweet bastard.

Who was nowhere in sight up here.

I looked beyond the edge of the roof and sucked in a breath at the sprawl of Vegas in all its glitzy, gaudy beauty: the imposing walls of the Mirage, the Eiffel Tower rising into the sky, and various fountains and pools glittering with sunshine." It's amazing up here."

Sam came up behind me, close enough for me to feel his heat, his exhalation on the curve of my neck. "Your world is so closed, Kate. So insular. Your apartment, your home office, and the drive here and back. The world is waiting right outside your door." He gestured to the city beyond. "Life is out there. All you have to do is grab it."

I spun around, indignation at his statement heating my cheeks. Instead, the fight wilted at seeing the gentle sympathy on his face. And something more. Deeper.

Love.

We had just exchanged those words when Oscar had burst onto my balcony and attacked him, accusing him of trying to kill me. And that had killed my hope for this odd triangle to work.

Sam brushed the hair from my face where the hot wind had washed it across my mouth. He tucked it behind my ears, a painfully familiar gesture. "I know you're doing the best that you can. I just want you to be happy."

I felt my body lean toward him. *Happy.* What was that? Oh, yeah, what I'd felt during those months I'd let myself fall in love with Sam and think we had a future. After that attack, I broke things off to save Sam, I'd told myself. To preserve Oscar's sanity.

Had I done it to keep myself safe too? Had I felt a twinge of relief at crawling back into my insular hole?

I couldn't think about that now, not with my brother contemplating suicide somewhere in this huge complex. "I became my brother's keeper because no one else would. Focusing on just that makes life simpler for everyone."

"Yeah, sure." But Sam's eyes called me on my bullshit.

"Where else could he be?" I asked, steering our conversation back to the matter at hand. I tried Oscar's phone again, but no luck. "Dammit, Oscar!" I said to his voice mail. "Call me!"

Sam was watching me with concern. "Maybe I should call my boss, mobilize—"

I stilled his hand before he could reach for the phone clipped to his waistband. "We have time. I don't want to officially involve security, because they'll have to call the police, and I know my brother. That would definitely push him over the edge. One time—he swears he wasn't trying to commit suicide—he walked out onto a ledge and someone called the police. He nearly fell because he got dizzy and stressed out by the authorities, and all the people who gathered to watch. We need to give this our best effort before we do that."

"You know him better than anyone else. I'll go with your judgment. And I agree, it's better if we—if you find him."

I wrapped my fingers around his forearm. "Thank you. You could have just handed me off to security, saved yourself a lot of trouble... "

"I told you, I'm tough. I can handle a lot. Especially when the stakes are worth it." He let those words settle into my heart for a moment. "Let's try a different tack and focus on execution. What methods has he used in his previous attempts?"

"I caught him trying to hang himself in the closet. That was the first attempt. The other time it was pills that he'd been stockpiling. I keep track of them, though I haven't been watching him take them now that he's been doing so well. He could have been stashing them. But hell, anyone can buy razor blades. Or rope."

"Those are the kinds of suicides people generally commit in a room, which is where a lot of them happen. Let's go back down to the lobby and see if he's checked in."

As soon as we were closed up in the staff elevator, he asked, "Why were you crying at night?"

"We don't have time for this."

"We do. And it plays into Oscar's thinking, so consider it part of our investigation."

I sigh, because he's probably already figured it out anyway. "Losing you hurt like hell. I knew that I'd made the right decision, but—"

"For who?" he demanded.

"For you. For Oscar."

"But not you."

I shook my head. "I knew it would be miserable for you and Oscar if we continued seeing each other, which would be miserable for me too. But that didn't make it any easier to lose you. Sometimes I'd wake in the night and it would just hit me all over again. About a month ago, Oscar barged in and blamed you for making me cry. I couldn't pretend anymore. I screamed that it was his fault." I covered my mouth. "I hope that didn't cause all of this. I just couldn't let him blame you anymore."

"Oh, babe," Sam said, reminding me of all the other times he'd used that endearment, when I *was* his babe.

The doors slid open, and I quickly moved away as two employees waited for us to depart.

Sam used both his security authority and his charm to persuade the clerk to check the computer without giving her a reason. No Oscar Simmons in the system. I was both relieved and despondent. Sheesh, maybe I *was* a little crazy.

Sam was already leading me away, calling someone on his phone. "Hey, it's Sam Kinkaid in security. Can you tell me if a janitorial employee had a reason to go into one of the rooms today... okay?" He whispered to me, "She's checking." A few seconds later, he turned back to the phone. "Yeah?... Okay, thank you, Marta." After disconnecting, he said, "She said it would be unusual for someone in the public cleaning sector to ask for access to a room, and she's fairly certain no one did, because she would have been consulted."

"Where are we going now?"

"Parking garage. Two years ago a woman jumped from the top level. The incident was part of my training."

"Training?"

"Nevada is among the highest states as far as suicide rates go, with Vegas being the place of choice—a fact that doesn't quite get mentioned in those tourist bureau ads. Casino security personnel get training on how to handle both an active attempt and the aftermath. So far I've only had to deal with two incidents: the woman I mentioned and a man from San Diego facing prison once his embezzlement was discovered. He did it in his room and left a note. It was a done deal by the time I arrived on the scene."

"Why do people go away to end their life?"

"I think in some cases it's so their family doesn't have to find their body. It's a stranger who has to deal with the discovery, and someone else's responsibility to clean the mess." He glanced at me. "Oscar loves you enough to free you; he'd save you that trauma."

"I can see that. During his lucid times, he feels bad for how he affects my life."

We both scanned the ground level of the parking garage as we walked briskly toward the elevator in the corner. Thank goodness there wasn't enough time for Sam to ask probing questions on the way up, since we weren't going very high. We spilled out of the car and took in the top level. It wasn't as vast as the roof, but I still couldn't see the whole deck because of the walls around the ramp.

"I'll take that side," I said, racing toward the far end.

"Check over the walls, just in case he already jumped." At seeing her cringe, he added, "Sorry, but we have to consider all possibilities."

"No, it's okay." He was used to talking about death in a matter-of-fact way. "It's a good idea."

Within a few minutes, we met in the middle, slightly breathless. I could see the disappointment in his face, as I'm sure he could see the fear building in mine.

He glanced at his watch. "We have two hours and five minutes." His expression reflected my own agony. Maybe not as much for Oscar, but for what his death would do to me. And I knew that Sam would do everything within his power to find Oscar, even though his death meant my freedom. That was the kind of man Sam was. My heart twisted with the depth of his feelings for me and the loss of him in my life.

"What if we're making a mistake by waiting to call in security?" I asked, torn by our two choices.

"We'll compromise." He made a call. "Bobby, it's Sam. I'm not on duty, but I want a low-key BOLO. Possible suicide." He gave a description of Oscar. "He's an employee, and he could be easily spooked, which is why we want to keep it on the down-low. If you see him, notify only me, and approach him as though you just want to chat. Keep him occupied. Thanks."

We spent the next hour and a half checking all of the back alleys of the hotel, the places only employees saw: kitchens, housekeeping, the janitorial department where Oscar worked. Nothing. We stopped into the security room filled with images from the myriad cameras hidden all over. We checked crammed closets, dusty storage rooms, and hot machinery rooms. Then all around the exterior of the buildings, ending where the Dumpsters lurked, along with two homeless people who were digging inside them despite the locked gates. Sam paused, probably knowing he should oust them. He didn't.

I loved this man. My heart swelled with it, even as it pumped fear through my veins for every passing minute that brought us closer to six. His calmness kept me from exploding. Someday I would tell him how wonderful he'd been on this terrible day. But I couldn't right then, because I'd fall apart.

Sam checked his watch again as we cruised through the front lobby. "We have twenty-nine minutes until his deadline."

I sagged onto one of the plush benches near the entrance, where the sun streamed in through the high windows. "Time to officially alert Excelsior security. I'll tell them that you only just now found out about this situation. I don't want you to get in trouble."

The sound of laughter pulled my attention to the right, where the sign read WEDDING CHAPEL. Voices floated out, a mash of several people, the words mostly indistinct. Something about flowers and noisemakers. A man laughed with a honking sort of sound. Two men and a woman, dressed casually nice, chatted as they rounded the corner and walked through the entrance draped in white chiffon.

"It seems wrong," I said, "that while my brother is preparing to end his life, people are celebrating a new chapter in theirs."

Sam was still staring at the entrance. We couldn't see into the room, because the entrance tilted at an angle.

I followed his gaze, my eyes narrowing. "We haven't looked in there, though I doubt he'd plan to do it in a chapel. Especially with a wedding about to go on."

Sam stood. "I said we'd check every inch of the public spaces before we give in. So we check there too. Then I make the call."

He took my hand again, silent support even when I didn't think I'd need it right then. In a minute he'd have to launch a full-scale search for a suicidal man. If we found Oscar in time, this would ruin any chance he had of retaining this job. Or his dignity.

Twenty or so people milled around inside the small room with rows of chairs strung with ribbons. Music played in the background, sweet and light. A few people glanced up, dismissed us as strangers, and returned to their conversations.

There was only one door in the room, with a sign that read CHAPEL STAFF ONLY. It was cracked open, and I saw people inside. Not a place Oscar would be.

Except... he was. The door swung open wider, and he stepped through. He wore a cheap suit, and he was talking with a man in a white tuxedo who looked official. More stunningly, he wore a broad smile as he held out his hand to a woman in a beige dress and a wispy veil that hung halfway down her back.

My knees buckled, and I gripped Sam's arm for balance. He was staring at Oscar too. Relief rushed through me like a hot Nevada wind, stealing my breath. Oscar wasn't going to kill himself. He was... *getting married?*

Just then he looked my way. Probably that twin thing. His smile faltered, then faded altogether. He pasted it back on as he released the woman's hand, murmuring something to her, and strode my way.

"What are you doing here?" he said with that same false cheeriness. "You two are supposed to be rolling around in bed."

Rage kicked in, quickly sweeping my relief to the side. "While I thought you were going to kill yourself?" I hissed.

He actually had the nerve to look perplexed. "Kill myself? Why would you think that?"

I pulled my phone from my purse and pulled up his text. My hand was shaking as I shoved it in his face. "What was I supposed to think?"

He whispered the words as he read, something he always did. "I said I was fine. Happy even." His face went pale. "Oh, yeah. I guess I can see why you thought that. Especially considering... "He glanced down for a second, then back up. "I'm sorry. I threw you for a tizzy again. This is what I wanted to avoid. Permanently. Didn't you get my letter?"

"What letter?" Sam and I asked simultaneously.

"The one I slid under your door when you didn't answer," he said to Sam.

Sam shook his head. "I didn't see any letter. But... the luggage is there. It must have slid beneath it."

"I explained it all there, though not the location." His smile bloomed over his face. "I'm getting married!"

"And you weren't going to invite your sister?" Sam asked, outraged on my behalf.

Oscar ignored him, focusing on me. "As I said, I knew you'd talk me out of it. And yes, it's hasty. I've only known Olivia a short time. Then again, you two fell in love fast, and I could see that it was real, even if I called it crazy love. That's why it scared me, because I knew things were going to change. That you'd probably send me off to a mental facility. And I wouldn't blame you." He glanced over at the woman watching our exchange. "This is the first time I've been in love, and I figured, if it happened like that for you, it could happen to me too."

I felt as though I'd been in a mental car wreck, sixty to zero in a screech of metal. "Are you doing this to free me? Be honest, Oscar. Marriage is serious business."

Oscar took my hands in his and beamed. "I'm doing it because I'm in love. Crazy love. The good kind of crazy. Olivia and I met in the support group. She's heading it, actually. She's a therapist who's battled bipolar herself. She understands me—all of us—better than we do. We've hit the sweet spot in my meds, and I feel... balanced. Clear-headed. Which is amazing, except that now I understand what I did to you." He flicked a sad glance to Sam. "To both of you. It was totally my fault you've been crying. I'm glad you told me that, because it made me think. And try harder. I read some of the caregiver books in your room, and I see how hard it's been on you." He gripped my hand. "Come, meet Olivia. You'll love her."

He included Sam in the invitation with his glance, leading me over to the woman who was clearly anticipating a row. As though I was the one prone to fits!

"Katie, I want you to meet Olivia Jones, my wife-to-be. Olivia, this is my sister, Katie, and her... her... well, the love of her life, Sam Kinkaid."

I went through the motions, nods, nice-to-meet-yous, shaking hands, all the while still trying to wrap my mind around this turn of events.

"I'm sorry we didn't tell you," Olivia said in a sweet, calm voice. "I told Oscar that he should, but he was adamant. He said you're more like a mother than a sister, which is normal in our situations. He was sure you would object. But now that you're here, we'd love for you to stay."

I turned to Oscar. "Are you sure? That you're ready?"

"Look, I know there will be ups and downs, but not like there have been. Olivia and I will keep each other in check, and our vows include to listen to the other person if they tell us we're going off the rails. We're committed. Now that I know how you felt about Sam, I'm even more torn up about what I destroyed. But it's not too late, right?" He looked at me, Sam, then me again.

Sam patted his arm. "I'm happy for you, bro." He gave me a pointed look. "Excuse me for a second. I have to call... *"Call off the BOLO.* Thankfully, he hadn't let Oscar know.

As soon as he stepped out of the chapel, Oscar squeezed my hands. "Tell me it's not too late. This is the last day of your deadline, right? He said he'd give you until tomorrow."

"He's already packed. Enlisted. But if he still feels the same, maybe we can do the long, long-distance thing until his tour is up." If he felt the same. The years of distance, the danger, I ached at the prospect of that, though. "We'll be fine. Go to your bride. Get married, with my blessing." I gave him a quick hug.

He tugged me toward the front, introducing me to the people in his group along the way. Names jumbled in my mind, but they were all genuinely happy for Oscar. They didn't think this was rash or wrong. I began to breathe easier.

Except for Sam. I kept glancing back as everyone took their seats and the happy couple stood at the front. Sam appeared in the doorway, and I beckoned him to sit next to me. The minister waited until he sat down and then began. No Elvis, but a woman dressed like an angel, complete with fluffy halo, waltzed in tossing confetti over the couple.

I picked it out of my hair as I watched my brother exchange vows, including the one he'd told me about, and kiss his bride. Everyone stood and clapped, and Oscar invited everyone to join them at the back of the room for festivities. Now that the adrenaline had drained from me, I sagged against Sam as everyone milled around, drinking non-alcoholic champagne. The couple had arranged a Lake Tahoe honeymoon. I gave them a hug and wished them well. Sam hugged the bride and shook hands with Oscar.

Thirty minutes later, the whole party had departed, a procession of cheers and more confetti. Sam steered me into the now empty chapel, guiding me down to a chair at the back.

"You all right?" he asked. "You look like you're about to faint, cry, and laugh all at once."

I did laugh. "That about sums it up." I hugged him, breathing in the scent of him, the feel of his body. "Thank you," I said, hoping those raw words conveyed my gratitude.

"Anything for you, Kate."

I gathered my courage and leaned back to look at his beautiful face. "You were right. I think I did use my brother's condition as a shield. Because right now I feel so completely vulnerable. Fragile. But a part of me knows I'm completely safe with you. And everything you did today proved it."

Now I touched his face, his lips. "I did cry, almost every night. Because I knew I'd given up the most wonderful, honorable, loving man I would ever meet. The only man for me. You waited for me, so I'll wait for you while you do this tour. Even though it will kill me to be apart from you, to know you'll be in danger. You're worth it, Sam. I love you so much."

He kissed me, tender and sweet, holding back the passion I knew lurked just beneath the surface. His fingers remained on my chin, his mouth close to mine, as he said, "I love you too. And I love that you would wait for me. But it's not necessary."

This was it. He was letting me down gently. "Oh. Does that mean…?"

"I didn't reenlist."

My heart stuttered. "What?"

"That was my plan, but my heart wasn't in it. Because I did still hope. For us. And when my boss offered me a promotion to security shift manager, I accepted. It was time to move out of here, so I rented an apartment."

Tears of joy finally released from the dam. "Well, there'll be one more change of plans. Tomorrow… you're moving in with me."

2

CHOOSING TO LOVE

The Griffin Brothers Origin Story

Crystal Perkins

1982

<u>Gary</u>

No one ever said getting a divorce was easy, but they also didn't say it would be this hard. I loved my wife in the beginning, but as her demands for more money and more prestige grew, my love started to wane. If it had been up to her, I would've taken the jobs I was offered and let her live in the lap of the luxury she felt she deserved. Instead of giving her what she wanted, I insisted on staying at the company that gave me a chance as a teenager. Loyalty has always been more important to me than money. Money will come one day—or it won't— but I'll never sell my soul for a dollar.

Cara's back in Chicago looking for a whale, while I'm here in Vegas with our six-year-old daughter, Erin. I have to be at this real estate conference in the Excelsior Hotel and Casino for work, but heaven forbid Cara could keep Erin with her for the week—it's not like she's her mother or anything. Yeah, I'm bitter, but not because she's sleeping her way to the top. I'm really and truly past that point. I just want her to act like a mother once in a while and put our daughter first.

"Daddy, is there a pool here?"

I crouch down to look her in the eye. "I'm sure there is Erin. Let's get checked in, and then we can take a look around."

"You have to go later," she reminds me, pouting.

"I do, but I have some time before then."

"What if I don't like the babysitter?"

"It's only for a few hours today. If you don't like her, we'll find someone new tomorrow."

"Can she take me to the circus if I like her?" she asks, referring to Circus Circus.

"We'll see."

I know it's 1982, not 1962, and that Vegas has been cleaning itself up, but I still don't like the idea of my little girl running around a city that was built by the mob—even if she's supervised. I'll talk to the girl the agency sends, and see what she thinks. Asking for her opinion is a good way to vet her as well as finding out how safe she thinks things are around here.

I check us in and am surprised when the key I'm given is to a large suite, not a standard room. I think it must be a mistake, until I see a giant fruit basket with my name on it. The card tells me that my bosses wanted us to have room to move around in, so they upgraded us. Just another little thing that lets me know I made the right decision in staying with them. One day, I want to own my own company— building and selling property all over Chicago—but for now, I'm happy with my choices. In my job and in my marriage, or rather the end of it.

Maggie

College degrees mean nothing if you can't find a job; I graduated a year ago and am working as a by-the-hour babysitter for the rich folks staying on The Strip instead of running a business somewhere. I don't know what kind of business I want to work for, or where I want to end up, but I want a chance, dammit. Despite all the television shows where the women are powerful and strong, here in the real world, companies aren't willing to take a chance on hiring a woman executive; at least not many of them.

I can't dwell on that as I prepare to knock on the door of this suite at the Excelsior. It's time to put on a bright smile and pretend I love my job. Some of the families I've sat for are decent enough, but I don't have high hopes for a single dad bringing his daughter to Vegas. And what if there is no daughter? I may not have been born here, but I've lived in Vegas long enough to know that things like this happen—

a fake job could lead to kidnapping, and worse. I grip the mace in the bottom of my purse, and knock on the door, ready for whatever might be on the other side.

When it swings open, I'm facing one of the most gorgeous men I've ever seen. Tall, with black hair, and bone structure Michelangelo would've killed to sculpt. It's his eyes that suck the breath from my lungs, those—piercing green eyes that seem to be probing my soul. I force myself to breathe normally under the scrutiny of this man who's only looking at me as a caretaker for his child, and not as a woman.

"Margaret?" he asks, as I stand there looking like a fool—great first impression I'm giving.

"It's Maggie," I tell him, finding my voice and holding out my hand. "Nice to meet you, Mr. Griffin."

"I'm Erin," a little girl says, coming to stand next to him.

She's got the same hair and eyes as her father, but while he's got on a suit and tie, she's got on a *Charlie's Angels* logo T-shirt and denim skirt. Her fashion choices alone make me love her a little. I crouch down to her level so I can greet her properly.

"I'm Maggie, and I love your T-shirt. My favorite Angel is Kelly."

"Mine too!"

"I would tell you to limit her television time, but I'm afraid she's already addicted."

"We'll do more than just watch TV," I assure him, as he opens the door wider so I can walk into the suite.

"We went to the pool today, Daddy. They had a slide. Have you seen it?"

"Yep. It's pretty cool."

"Erin can swim, but I don't want her left unattended."

"Of course not."

"She would also like to see the circus down the street. Is it safe to walk down there?"

"I wouldn't suggest it at night with a little girl, no. We can take the bus or taxi, or you could get a car from the hotel."

He looks conflicted before he answers. "Do *you* have a car?"

I do have a car, but no one's ever asked me to use it. "It should be safe, but yes, I have a car."

"I would pay you gas if you'd drive her."

"We can work something out, sure."

"Thanks. I should get going. You're okay staying here with Maggie, right Erin?"

She walks over and wraps her hand around mine. "I like her."

"Great."

"Um, Mr. Griffin?"

"Huh?"

"Are we ordering room service?" That's what usually happens when I sit at the hotels, especially when the parents are staying in one of these suites.

"Oh, no. I mean, we passed some casual food places downstairs when we were going to the pool. I think those would be better."

"Sure. We can go downstairs."

"Do I give you money now, or do you add it to my bill?" he asks, reaching for his wallet.

"You can pay me later." I can afford one meal. More than one may be a problem, but I'll deal with that if it comes up.

"Perfect," he tells me before picking his daughter up in a big hug. "You know the rules, so don't try to break any just because I don't have time to tell Maggie everything."

"Would I do that?" she asks, batting her eyes as I laugh.

He tweaks her nose, and then puts her down. "Yeah, you would like totally do that."

I laugh even harder at his "valley" speak, and when I meet his gaze, his eyes are twinkling in amusement. "Have fun," I say as he walks out the door.

Gary

Smiling and shaking hands gets tedious after five hours. Especially when I already did it last night as well. I grin and bear it because it's something I have to do if I want to get the company I work for more contracts, which will then get me bigger bonuses. Maybe even enough to splurge on a car rental to drive my daughter around instead of asking her sexy babysitter to do it.

Whoa! Where the hell did that thought come from? I can't think of Maggie like that, not just because she's several years younger than me, but because she *is* the babysitter. Erin was sound asleep when I got back last night, but she couldn't stop gushing about Maggie this morning. So yeah, I shouldn't be lusting over her, but damn if I can stop, even when I'm being presented with plenty of other offers.

"Hi, Gary," one of the women who not-so-subtly offered herself to me last night after we meet at the conference says, as she walks up behind me.

"Hi."

"Since this is our free night, I was hoping we could get together for dinner, or even just dessert."

I'm all for women's empowerment, but when she reaches her hand down to grab my ass, I move away. She tilts one of her shoulders, causing one of her shoulder pads to go askew. It takes a ton of self-control to maintain a straight face, but I do.

"I'm spending time with my daughter tonight."

"I'm sure you could spare some time for me."

"Really, I can't. I'm sorry." No, I'm not.

"Do you know who my father is?"

Yes, I know. I'm not willing to trade sex for jobs, even if I do need the money. The fact that she suggested it makes me want her even less. "Have a good conference," I say as I walk away. Dodged a bullet there.

The rest of the day passes in a blur of schmoozing, and eating the superb food the hotel is providing for the conference. I feel a little guilty thinking about how I've been dining on steak and lobster while Erin and Maggie had pizza last night, but I can't afford to buy this kind of food. Actually, that's not true. I could afford it, but I'd rather put the money in Erin's college fund, and make some much needed repairs to our house. I have no problem sacrificing for my girl, which is why it feels so wrong to be living the high life without her. When I think about it that way, it sucks, but then I remember I'm doing this for both of us, and that's what's really important.

The suite is empty when I get there, so I switch into jeans and a T-shirt while I wait for my girls to get back. Shit, I need to stop that. Erin is mine, but Maggie isn't. I don't know if she has a guy, but with her long brown hair, gorgeous face, and curvy body, I doubt she's making desperate plays for guys anywhere.

I'm going over some proposals for tomorrow when the door opens and they come rushing in. "Hey, ladies."

"Daddy!" Erin runs over throwing her slender arms around me. "We had so much fun today! The circus was fun, and then we had lunch downtown. I got two corn dogs!"

"Downtown?" I ask, knowing I didn't approve that.

"It was safe," Maggie says, but she can't look me in the eye.

"Erin, honey, why don't you go into your room and take a little nap while I talk to Maggie."

"Don't be mad at her, Daddy! I love her!"

Well, this just got more complicated. "I only want to talk to her, so please go to your room."

She hugs Maggie tight, and I'm not sure she'll let her go. Maggie pulls herself free, and whispers in her ear. She looks at me one more time, begging me with her eyes to be nice, but I can't promise that right now.

"You didn't have permission to take her downtown," I say through clenched teeth once Erin's door is closed.

"She needed to eat," she says softly.

"There were no places at Circus Circus?"

"I-I couldn't afford any of the restaurants there, okay? Eating downtown is cheap. Not all of us in this room are rich," she tells me, playing with the rubber bracelets on her wrists.

Shit. Now I feel like an even bigger asshole. "I'm sorry. I should've left some money for you. And for the record, *none* of us in this room are rich," I reply.

"You're in this suite."

"My bosses paid for it since I'm here in their place at the conference."

"Conference? You're here for a conference?"

"Yeah. What, did you think I brought my daughter here while I was gambling and fucking around?" I ask with a laugh, but she doesn't join in.

"Yes."

"Wow. You have a really high opinion of me, huh?"

"I don't know you well enough to have an opinion. I shouldn't have judged you, but usually people who call me to come to a suite want me to distract their kids while they play."

"That's not me. I love my job, but I'd spend all day, every day with Erin, if I could."

"I should probably go now."

"You'll be here tomorrow, won't you? I really am sorry."

"How could I stay away from Erin?"

"You couldn't."

"See you tomorrow, Mr. Griffin."

"Gary."

"Goodnight," she says, not acknowledging me telling her to call me by my first name. I'm going to hear her say it, because damn if I don't want her to say it. I'm on a sinking ship, but I think she could be my life boat, even if it's just for the rest of the week.

Maggie

I'm more nervous today than I was two days ago as I approach Gary's suite. He told me to call him Gary, and damn if I don't want to. I shouldn't, but I do. I can't get involved with him. I'm already way too involved with Erin, but how could I not be? Her father is another matter—one I need to stay far away from.

"Hi, Maggie," the sexy man in question says, answering the door.

He's got his jacket off and his tie's not on yet. I want to lick his neck where it's exposed from the button that's undone. That little triangle of skin looks too damn lickable, but I can't do it. I can't have him, no matter how much I want him. I've seen other sitters fall under a spell, and then sit around eating ice cream for days when the guy leaves. I have enough on my mind without worrying about a broken heart.

"Hello, Mr. Griffin."

"Maggie, I told you to call me Gary."

"I don't think that's a good idea."

"Why not?" he asks, moving closer to me.

"You're my boss," I breathe out as he lifts his hand to my cheek.

"Daddy's going to be everyone's boss one day. Not soon enough for Mommy, but one day," Erin says, breaking us out of whatever was about to happen. I need to buy her an ice cream cone for that.

"One day," he tells her, making me wonder just what happened between him and his ex-wife. At least I assume it's an ex.

"Are you divorced?" I blurt out, and then slam my hand over my mouth.

"I am," he tells me as he buttons that button, then puts his tie on. "Is that a problem?"

"No. Of course not."

"I'll see you girls tonight," he says, putting his jacket on and heading for the door. "Oh, I almost forgot. Here's some cash for lunch."

"Oh, we don't need that," I tell him, patting my bag. "I made us some lunch for today."

"You didn't have to," he says, looking pained.

"I wanted to. Now go on before you're late. You can't be the boss of everyone if you're late."

"No, I guess not. Thanks, Maggie."

"You're welcome, Gary."

I don't even realize I've said it until his eyes go wide and he smiles at me. Damn it, I wasn't going to do that. I was *never* going to do it. He nods at me, and then he's gone.

"Do you like my Daddy?" Erin asks me when he's gone.

"Of course. He's a very nice man."

"Can you come to Chicago and be my babysitter? We have two extra bedrooms and there's lots of closet space now that Mommy left."

"I wish I could, but I need to find a job."

"Babysitting me is your job. You said so."

"It is, but it's not the job I went to college for."

"What job is that?"

"I want to run a business one day, or at least help someone run their business."

"Daddy wants his own business, but he's not ready yet. That's why Mommy left—she said she needed... " She paused, thinking, then recites: "Valentino gowns and fur coats. I think fur coats are icky!"

"Me too," I tell her, trying to process what she just told me, which also fits with something he said—her mother left Gary because he's not rich.

"Can we go to the pool now?"

"Yeah, sure. Let's get you in your suit, and then we'll head on down."

All I can think about while we're changing is that Gary is a good man, and yeah, a pretty fine one too. How someone could leave him is beyond me, because I wouldn't kick him out of my bed. I know he'll never be in my bed, but still. Stupid, stupid woman for leaving him—and stupid me for even thinking about him and a bed in the same sentence.

Gary

"Do you have a date for the gala tonight?" the woman I just can't seem to shake asks as she once again tries to grab my ass.

I step to the side, and speak without thinking. "Yes, I do."

"Really? Who is it?"

"No one you know. She's local, and not with the conference."

"What's her name?" she asks, her eyes getting narrower with every question.

"Maggie," I blurt out, because I just like digging my holes deeper and deeper apparently.

In my defense, we're outside the conference room on a terrace overlooking the pool, and I can't help but feel like a cornered antelope trying to escape from the lioness who's hunting me. I can always make up a reason as to why Maggie couldn't attend, but right now, I'm just trying to come away from this conversation unscathed.

"Where did you meet this mystery woman?"

"Here in the hotel."

"I haven't seen you in any of the bars or lounges," she tells me, moving closer as I circle away from her.

I'm trying to come up with an explanation when the woman in question appears. "Hi, Gary."

"Maggie," I sigh, thanking the heavens for bringing her to me. Now—bringing her to me right now, I mean. And wow. She's in a black bathing suit that's strapless on top, but has straps and sheer panels covering her middle in a cool pattern. She's covered, but also the sexiest thing I've seen in my life.

"Aren't you going to introduce us?" the other woman asks.

"Oh, um, yeah. Maggie this is..." Shit. I have no idea what this woman's name is.

"Unbelievable! I've been making myself available to you for the last two days and you don't know my name? You do business with my father!"

"I know your father's name," I answer with what I hope is an apologetic look on my face.

She storms off and I turn to Maggie. "Thanks for that."

"You looked like you needed help."

"I did, but where's Erin?"

"Oh, a couple of the guys I know offered to watch her for a few minutes," she says, gesturing behind her to where I see my little girl playing with some guys. Athletic looking guys I recognize. Holy shit!

"Are those the Lakers?"

"Some of them," she says with a shrug.

"You know them?"

"Kind of. They've been here when I've been babysitting before. We're more of acquaintances."

"How many have hit on you?" Did I just say that out loud?

She raises an eyebrow at me, letting me know, that yes, I did ask her that. "All of them."

I nod, and then remember that I kind of need to hit on her. The wood I'm trying to hide behind my suit jacket is affecting my brain, but how could I help it? She's standing in front of me with wet fabric clinging to every one of her luscious curves; I'm only human.

"What if I was to hit on you?"

"Excuse me?"

"No. Not really. I mean, you're gorgeous, but I know we can't. I mean, I accidentally told that woman you're my date for the gala tonight."

"Oh."

"Can you... would you?"

"Yes, um, we would have to get someone else to watch Erin, but I have friends who would do it."

"I'll pay you, of course, and buy you a dress if you need one."

"I'm not a hooker!"

"What? No. I didn't mean it like that. It's just, you shouldn't be forced to go with me and get nothing in return."

"Maybe I'll get exactly what I want in return."

Oh. She's got a look in her eyes that I want to believe is lust. I want that so fucking bad, because if she really wants me, she can have me.

"I have to get back to my meetings."

"And I have to get ready for tonight. I'll see you later."

"Yeah, see you later, and thanks. Again."

"You're welcome," she says, moving closer and kissing me softly on the lips. Then she pulls away slowly and whispers, "Your friend was watching."

Maggie

I take Erin from the guys, who are having as much fun playing with her as they seem to do on the court—it's no wonder, she's an awesome girl. I also fend off a few more advances with a smile, and hold her hand as we walk inside.

"Why did we have to leave so soon?" she asks while yawning.

"We've been there for two hours, and it's time to eat. Then I have to get ready to go to a gala with your dad!"

"Like a ball?"

"Pretty much."

"You can dance with Daddy, and fall in love."

"We don't know each other well enough to fall in love." Lie. I am a liar, and I know it. I didn't believe in love at first sight until I met Gary Griffin, but yeah, I'm pretty sure I'm in love with him—or at least really deep like.

"You kissed him." This kid misses *nothing*.

"He needed my help." Yep, that's why I did it—it was not at all because I needed to have my mouth on his.

"I think he likes you too. He's happy when he sees you."

"I think we need to get going before I end up having wet hair for the gala. No one would want to kiss me if I look like I have seaweed for hair!"

She giggles at that, which is just what I was going for. I need to keep this light, and fun, because even if Gary is happy to see me, that doesn't mean he wants more than a date for the gala. He needs my help, and I'll give it to him, but I won't expect anything else.

Once Erin and I have finished the sandwiches and chips I brought for us, I start to call in the favors I need. My best friend's mom runs the designer dress shop here in the hotel, my college roommate is a hairdresser in the salon here, and *her* best friend is a makeup artist for the burlesque show. They all agree to help, and I make a last call to my best friend, Taz, getting her to agree to watch Erin tonight.

Erin and I both get primped and pampered for the rest of the afternoon. Her hair is curled, while mine is teased and crimped until I look like a hair commercial come to life. My makeup is all shades of pink, but not quite as extreme as what the showgirls rock. I look and feel beautiful, and now all I need is my dress, shoes, and jewelry.

We're in a room my friends got comped for me, and I practically jump for joy when the knock at the door comes. The dress

Taz's mom brings me is fun, flirty, and expensive. Seriously, it costs almost as much as I make in a year, and I'm scared to put it on. In the end, I relent, because I love it. A strapless, scalloped black bodice leads into asymmetrical rows of still and pleated ruffles in hot pink and purple that flow to the floor. It's a little snug over my boobs, but fits perfectly everywhere else.

"I hate your cleavage," Taz tells me, and I just laugh and hug my bestie. "And I hate your gorgeous skin and hair, so we're even."

I slip into the hot pink heels I'm given, and attach the large angel wing earrings to my ears, but I shake my head at the long gloves. I only have this one night to be with my prince, and I want to feel his hand in mine with no barrier. I spin in circles as Erin plays with the taffeta ruffles and jumps up on the bed so she can hug me tight.

"You look like a princess."

"That's the best compliment anyone's ever given me."

"I think we should get going, before your dad starts wondering where we are," Taz tells her.

"We'll tell Daddy where to find you," Erin assures me.

"Thanks."

Everyone clears out, and I'm left alone with my thoughts. I still don't know what I'm doing, or what I'm going to *do*. This is supposed to be just a job, but Gary—and Erin—have brought out feelings in me I didn't know I had. I want them both, but I know it's not an option. Gary is getting over a divorce, and I don't want to give up my dreams for a man. For this one night, I'm going to let all of this go, but I know the real world will be back tomorrow.

Gary

I hear the outer door open, and walk out of my bedroom, expecting to see Maggie and Erin. Erin is there, but the woman with her isn't my date for tonight. "Hello, you must be Maggie's friend."

"Yes, I'm Taz," she says, crossing her arms over her chest as she looks me over.

"Daddy, look at my pretty hair and fingernails," Erin tells me, pulling on the leg of my tux.

"You look absolutely divine, my love," I tell her with a smile.

"Like pretty?"

"It's better than pretty," I say, as I tweak her nose.

"Oh. Wait 'til you see Maggie. She looks super divine."

"I have no doubt."

"Can I speak to you alone for a moment, Mr. Griffin?" Taz asks me.

"Yes, of course, and you can call me Gary."

"I know, I know—go to my room, please," Erin says, rolling her eyes, before heading to her room and closing the door.

"I'll come in and say goodbye before I leave."

Once she's out of earshot, I turn to Maggie's friend, waiting for the inquisition. She doesn't disappoint. "I don't like you messing with Maggie."

"I'm not."

"She likes you."

"I like her too."

"You're using her."

"For the gala, yes. Other than that, I have no intention of using her."

"You want to have sex with her."

"I won't deny it," he says, after deciding her intent.

"Just be straight with her, okay. She doesn't sleep around."

"I don't sleep around, either, and I'm nothing if not a straight shooter."

"Good. She's downstairs in room 1010. My mom got her the room for the whole night, and I can stay over here."

"Thank you, Taz."

"Go say goodbye to Erin, and then run your butt downstairs—my friend doesn't deserve to be kept waiting. I've got dinner covered."

She doesn't have to tell me twice. I spend a few minutes with Erin, and while I don't run to Maggie, I *do* walk briskly to the elevator. It seems to take forever to make it down to her floor, when I know it's less than a minute. I just can't wait to see her.

I jog to her door, and knock, thinking about that soft kiss she gave me. It may have only been for show, but I loved it. Hell, I'm pretty sure I loved that little peck on the lips more than I've loved any other kiss in my entire life. I don't know what's going on here, or why I feel like I might already be falling for her when we've only known each other for two days, but I need her lips on me again.

The door opens, and I stagger backwards. She's in a black, pink, and purple dress, her hair is crinkly and big, and yeah, I'm just blown away. "Fuck."

"Oh no! Is this dress not okay? I have a back-up! I can change!"

"What? No. No. Please don't change. You look amazing."

"Really?"

"God, yes."

"Okay. You look very handsome in your tux."

"Handsome enough for another kiss?"

"That might be an option later."

Later? Well, damn. "I'll be holding out hope."

"Please do."

She takes my arm, and I lead us back the way I came. I know this is happening, but part of me believes it can't be. I'm an almost twenty-eight-year-old divorced single parent, and Maggie... Maggie is an insanely gorgeous and fun girl who can't be older than twenty-two. This could go all kinds of wrong, but what if it's exactly right?

Maggie

When we enter the ballroom, my nerves kick up again. Even though I know Gary isn't wealthy, I can tell most of the other attendees are. Thank God for my friends, and a borrowed designer dress—I'd be running back out if I didn't look the part I'm here to play. I can't help but grip Gary's arm tighter as we walk in.

Gary smiles. "Relax. I'm the luckiest bastard in the room right now, and every other guy here knows it."

"I'd say I'm pretty lucky too."

"Thanks for the compliment," he tells me, stopping to grab two glasses of champagne from a passing waiter. "Champagne?"

"Of course. When in Rome... "

We don't get more time to talk as it seems like half the room descends on us. The woman compliments my dress while glaring at me, and the men eye my tits, while Gary pulls me closer into his side. Dinner service starts soon after, and while we're sitting with nice people, I really wish we were alone. I want to talk to Gary more, because every piece of information he imparts, or every joke he makes, strengthens my attraction to him. I need to have my hands on him, and I need that soon.

"Would you like to dance?" he asks me.

"Yes," I say, practically jumping out of my seat when he pulls my chair out.

He holds me close to Chicago's *Hard to Say I'm Sorry*, and I can feel his heart beating as fast as mine is. "I don't want to presume anything, but are you ready to leave?"

"Definitely," I tell him, knowing he means more than he's saying. "We can go to my room."

"You're sure?"

"I am."

We finish the song and say our goodbyes as we calmly walk from the room. We hold hands as we ride up in the elevator, but that's all we do. It's not until we get inside my room that we let go of the control we've been holding onto.

Our mouths collide, our hands explore. It's magical and wonderful, and when he unzips my dress, I step out of it and take off his jacket. We kiss, touch, and fumble each other's clothes off, finally rolling onto the bed, where he takes me to new heights of ecstasy all night long.

Gary

Other than the day Erin was born, I can't remember feeling as happy as I do when I wake up with Maggie in my arms. She's cuddled up to my side, and I want to keep her there forever. The sex last night was phenomenal, but what I'm feeling is so much more than that, and I've decided to stop fighting it.

Since it's still early, I kiss her awake, swallowing her sweet moans and trying to ignore my hardening dick. "Good morning, beautiful."

"Morning. Do we have to get up?"

"No, but I was hoping we could talk before I go upstairs."

"Okay," she says, blinking her eyes as she smiles up at me.

"I've never felt like this before, Maggie, and I'll admit that it scares me a little. We barely know each other, but I feel more for you than the woman I married eight years ago."

"I feel it too."

"I want to know you, Maggie. Tell me all about you. Please."

"Well, I was born in Wisconsin, but we moved around a lot because my dad was in the military. I ended up going to UNLV on scholarship, and now I'm here."

"What did you major in?"

"Business Management, with an Econ minor. Summa cum laude."

"Why aren't you working for some big company? You're obviously brilliant."

"I have breasts and a vagina, in case you didn't notice."

"If you don't think I noticed, I did something wrong last night—and early this morning."

"If you did anything more 'right' I'd be in a coma right now. Seriously, though, not many big companies want women running them."

"Stupid men. If I had a company, I'd hire you in a heartbeat."

"Thanks. Now tell me all about yourself, Mr. Griffin."

I cringe at the name, until she kisses the frown from my face, and then motions for me to answer. I don't think I could ever deny her anything, so I do as I'm told. "I was born and raised in Chicago, and I always knew I wanted to build, buy, and sell buildings. I worked for the company I'm with now while I was in high school, and they hired me back once I left the Navy."

"You were in the Navy? Did you build things?"

"Yes, and no, I didn't build things. I was a SEAL."

"I had sex with a Navy SEAL? Damn, that's hot. We need to do that again once you're done talking, because I think my ovaries are exploding right now."

"Didn't get your fill of military guys when you were a teen?"

"I didn't think military men were cool when I was young because my dad was one, and I was bitter about moving around. Now? I can appreciate a nice ass in uniform."

"My ass looks good in a uniform," I tell her with a growl. I don't like the thought of her looking at other guys. At all.

"It looks better out of one, but keep talking. I want to know it all."

"You mean you want to know about Cara."

"Erin's mom?"

"Yes. We dated senior year of high school, and she thought it was 'cool' that I wanted to enlist. She wrote to me, and we spent my leaves together. After four years together, we got married and had Erin.

My being in the service stopped being exciting to her, so I left, thinking I could save our marriage. When I went to work for the guys at my current job instead of taking a more prestigious position somewhere else, she was very upset. I thought she'd get over it, but she didn't. She was never happy being middle-class, and when her last attempt to force me into a 'better' job failed, she left."

"Wow, what a bitch."

"Exactly."

"Do you miss her?"

"Hell no. Erin and I are better off without her."

"She doesn't spend time with Erin?"

"Not unless it will benefit her somehow. She wouldn't keep her this week, either."

"I would say I hate her, but if she'd kept Erin, we wouldn't have met."

"I know. I was thinking it too. I guess I have two things to thank her for now."

"I don't want this to end."

"Me neither. I have two days left here in Vegas, and we need to talk later. Right now, I have to get ready to go upstairs."

"Do you think we might have time for a shower?" She winks suggestively.

"I think you might be right." I tell her as I pull her up, and throw her over my shoulder. What a way to start the day!

Maggie

Gary and I manage to compose ourselves before we get to his hotel room. We agreed to not act differently in front of Erin yet, but I get one last peck on the mouth before he opens the door. My smile drops when I see a well-dressed woman sitting on the couch. Erin is sitting on Taz's lap in a chair, while her mother files her nails. I know it's Cara, because she jumps up and throws her arms around Gary, practically knocking him over.

"Lover, where were you? And why are you in a tux?"

I had a change of clothes downstairs, but Gary didn't. I guess the cat's out of the bag—or not. "Some of the guys started a poker game, and I joined in. It turned into an all-nighter."

"You and your poker games. My husband loves them," she says, finally noticing me. "And who are you?"

"I'm the daytime babysitter, Maggie."

"I'm your ex-husband, and what are you doing here, Cara?" I can hear the agitation in his voice.

"I came to be with my family. We won't need you today," she says, never shaking my outstretched hand. Well, this is beyond awkward.

"Taz and I should get going since we're not needed. Have fun with your mommy today, Erin."

I manage to hold onto my fake smile as I hug that little girl, and hold my head up as I walk out the door with my best friend. "Just put one foot in front of the other, Mags. You've got this."

"He didn't even try to stop me from leaving."

"I know. In his defense, she's a real piece of work. She barely hugged Erin, and then ignored her the entire time she was waiting for Gary. That sweet girl deserves better."

"Do you think that's it? He's just getting rid of her."

"It's what I want to believe."

Me too.

We go downstairs and clear out my stuff from the room. Taz was going to do it for me, but since I'm not needed upstairs, there's no reason for her to do that now. We get everything packed up, when there's a knock at the door. I open it, expecting to find her mom picking up my borrowed dress, but it's Gary and Erin instead.

"Hi."

"Hi."

"Can we come in?"

"Okay."

"My mommy went home," Erin tells me. "Will you stay with me today?"

"She's gone already?" I ask Gary.

"She shouldn't have been here in the first place, since she's not wanted—at least not by me. She's Erin's mother, so she's welcome to visit with advance notice, but she can't just show up."

"Oh."

"So you'll stay with me?" Erin asks.

"Of course I will."

"I'll wait for my mom," Taz tells me.

"Thanks."

The ride back upstairs is filled with Erin talking about what she wants to do today, and me working hard to ignore Gary. He sent Cara away, but I still feel embarrassed about what happened earlier, and how he let me walk out. I'm nobody's dirty secret. Not now, not ever.

Gary

I wanted to talk to Maggie this morning, but Erin was already freaked out by Cara's sudden appearance and departure, and I didn't want to send her to her room. I figured I'd talk to Maggie tonight, but I got invited to dinner by some important clients, and I was only able to call up the suite and tell them I wouldn't be back until late. Maggie told me it was fine, but I could tell she was still upset with me. Hell, I'm fucking upset with me too. I should've said something... anything. No, not anything. I should've claimed Maggie, because God knows I want to keep her. I wimped out, and now I need to make it up to her.

I splurged on some overpriced flowers and candles from one of the gift shops, and I brought back some wine and chocolate cake from the restaurant—and some milk for Erin. I want my daughter to be here while I woo Maggie, because I'm hoping she'll be a big part of our future.

When midnight rolls around, and they're still not back, I start to worry. I'm about to go down and look for them when the front door opens, Magic Johnson walks in with Erin in his arms. Another player walks in next to Maggie, and it takes every ounce of strength I have to keep my anger in check.

"You can put her in there," Maggie says, motioning the guy into the other room. "Thanks for helping us get back here."

"Anytime, Mags. We'll see you tomorrow—or I guess it's today."

"Probably," she tells him, giving them each a hug. "Thanks again."

They walk out and I spin her around to look at me. "What the fuck was that?"

"Do not speak to me that way."

"You show up here with some jocks, one of whom has my daughter in his arms, and you think you have the right to tell me what tone to use with you?"

"Yes."

"Well then, by all means, explain yourself."

"You're an asshole."

"And you are my employee. Tell me what happened, or I'll call your boss and find out from him."

She looks at me like I've slapped her, but I can't be sorry right now. This is my daughter we're talking about, and no one—not even Maggie—can come before her.

"A friend of mine got us tickets to see Siegfried & Roy at the Stardust. We had fun, but my car wouldn't start. The guys were at the show too, so they let us ride in their limo back to the hotel. Erin fell asleep, so Magic carried her up for me."

"What if they hadn't been there? You would've been stranded in the middle of the night with my daughter."

"We wouldn't have been stranded. I was going to go inside and call someone to pick us up."

"She wouldn't have been safe, either way."

"You honestly think I would've let anything happen to that little girl? I love her. I love—" she starts to say, but stops herself, which is for the best.

"Your services are no longer needed, Maggie."

"Can I come by in the morning and say goodbye to her?"

"No. I think it's better... for all of us... if you just go."

"Okay. Would you like me to send another sitter for tomorrow, Mr. Griffin?"

"Yes, please."

She walks out, and once again, I don't try and stop her. And this time, I'm not sorry.

Maggie

"What do you mean, she's missing?" I ask Trina. She's watching Erin today, and she just called the office to say she lost her.

I'm white knuckling the receiver as I listen to her tell me that they went down to the pool, and when Trina went to use the restroom, she came back to find her gone. I'm going to kill her. Like, seriously, take her out to the desert and leave her body.

"Why did you leave her there alone?"

"She said she wouldn't go in the pool."

"I'm on my way there. You better hope we find her."

The office is a few blocks from the Excelsior, and I run there in ten minutes—literally run there since I don't have my car back yet. It's ten minutes too long, but I wasn't going to wait for an unreliable bus.

I'm breathing heavily when I run inside, but most of it is from fear, and not the run. I stop short when I see Erin in Gary's arms. Thank you, God. I mean, really, really thank you for keeping her safe. I turn to walk away but her voice stops me.

"Maggie!" she screams before pulling away from her dad and running to me. I meet her halfway, and lift her into my arms. "I got lost. I was so scared."

"Where were you, honey? Why didn't you wait for Trina?"

"I had to pee too. I didn't have to go when she left, but then I did. I couldn't wait for her to get back, or I'd have an accident."

I put her down and kneel in front of her, cupping her face with my hands. "If something like that ever happens again, you have an accident, okay?"

"Big girls don't have accidents!"

"Sometimes they do. When they're trying to be safe, they do whatever they can to protect themselves."

"I love you, Maggie. I want you to come home with me to Chicago. Please can you do that?"

"I love you too, Erin, but I can't go with you."

"Not even if we both ask you?"

I look up at Gary, and try to hold my emotions in check. "I thought you never wanted to see me again."

"I was scared—for both of you—and I didn't handle it well. It's hard to be sensible when you think the two people you love most in the world are in danger."

"You... love me?"

"More than anything, except that little girl down there with you. I was going to call you tonight and apologize. I'm so sorry for everything, Maggie. I know you'll always make sure Erin's safe. I acted so badly to you—more than once."

"Yes, you did."

"Can you forgive me?"

"And be my new mommy?"

"You have a mommy, Erin," I remind her.

"You could be her step-mommy," Gary says, and my heart starts racing even faster.

"Are you asking me to marry you?"

"Yeah, that's exactly what I'm doing."

"We've only known each other for four days."

"Some of the best—and worst—days of my life. I think we can tip the scales to best if we try hard enough."

"You're serious."

"There's a jewelry store and a wedding chapel here. I couldn't be more serious. I may be bankrupt, but I want to make you my wife tonight."

"I can get us a discount on a ring, and the wedding. I don't need anything fancy, anyway."

"Is that a yes?"

"Yes, Mr. Griffin, it is."

3

THE WAY YOU LOOK TONIGHT

Amanda McIntyre

Aidan stared into the flames. It had been years, no, centuries since he'd felt her body beneath his. Her dark hair—a tumble of sensuous curls—splayed across his pillow, her smile teasing, taunting him. Even now, he grew hard to think of the scent of her skin, the taste of her lips. He swallowed, tamping down his frustration. She plagued his thoughts and haunted his dreams as she'd done for an eternity. And he had more of the same torture to look forward to.

He dropped his book on the floor and leaned forward, fisting his hands over his knees. Reading had always been a good deterrent for him, giving his mind something else to think about, but after literally decades, he'd read and re-read all the classics. Most recently, he'd been forced to find other books, having to try mysteries, horror, even paranormal—though he had to chuckle at their world-building descriptions. Vampyre held his interest for a time, but soon they made him homesick for Carpathia, and hungry to feel Lucynda's body writhing in perfect rhythm to his.

He'd immigrated to the Carpathian mountain region with his Celt parents when he was only a young man. One day, in search for food for his starving village, he ventured deeper than he should into the wood. The path twisted and turned. He became disoriented and stumbled upon a crumbling shack, hidden by a grove of trees. A fierce storm lashed rain across his flesh as he fought through the thickened weeds to get to the door. Much to his surprise, he was greeted by a beautiful, fair-haired woman who invited him in. She gave him a dry place to rest his head, a blanket for warmth and in the middle of the night she came to him, seduced him and set him on a path of becoming a creature of the night. He fought his primal urges for as long as he could, wandering the woods, joining with a secret society of Carpathian Vampyres who tutored him in his first kill and taught him how to survive.

It was several centuries later, when Aidan ran across an ad in a newspaper advertising the sale of a prime piece of real estate deep in the heart of the Las Vegas strip. It was the perfect camouflage for his lifestyle. Plenty of chaos. Plenty of people willing to do anything to make it. In some ways, building his empire here seemed too easy. Thus far, no one had questioned how Louis "The Lip" LaFica managed to have such a long line of heirs to his Excelsior hotel and all of its opulence. He lay in eternal sleep, deep inside a vault in the bowels of the hotel. Comforted in the knowledge that his reign as kingpin of Vegas would live forever through Aidan, his successor.

Aidan was in the prime of his reign. This was *his* city. In all its sinful glory. Given time and study, he'd managed to perfect the art of time travel so that during his feed, he'd be able to travel back and forth undisturbed, unnoticed. Louis would be impressed.

Restless, Aidan stood and stretched his arms over his head. It was a little over a week to the full moon. He grew bored waiting in his nest above the bright lights. Maybe he'd go work out or run down to see Oscar, his tattoo guy just off the strip. Longest living tattoo artist in the city. Aidan smiled, glad to have invested in that business venture. The man was brilliant, enormous control and a connoisseur of blood type and had the habit of chewing Clove Gum incessantly.

Cloves and cinnamon. *Lucynda.*

The pungent spices jarred his memory. He gazed out over the bustling city, lost in his thoughts, remembering the night he found her—or rather, she'd found him.

"Dames. Hard to shake the good ones from your memory." Frank, one of the more recent residents of the Excelsior sat down in a chair facing the plate glass panoramic view that was once his playground. "This helps some." His blue eyes, a signature as much as his Jack Daniels, glinted in the wash of neon light. He lifted his glass in salute and went back to his silent watch.

Aidan had known Frank since 1998. Before him, came Dean in '95, Sammy in '90, Pete was the first in '84, Joey the last in 2007. They resided now in the Excelsior. Possessing a power so strong in this town, it couldn't be quenched. They showed up one at a time in his bar after their old haunt, the Sands was demolished. Aidan set them up in the penthouse suites on the upper floors of the Excelsior. He liked to think that he'd become an unofficial member of the Rat Pack.

"That's life, right?" He slanted his friend a grin. Still, as he shared the view, he allowed his thoughts to wander back to when he'd found her... or rather, she'd found him. It'd been a quick trip to Britannia. His need for something from the Homeland—decidedly Scottish.

***

The air was sucked from his lungs as Aidan raised his head. His eyes met the wide-eyed gaze of the beautiful woman. He'd never seen such raven hair. It made his fingers itch to think of it sliding through his palms. Unfortunately, what she'd witnessed was not a clean kill and worse, the subject had struggled. He thought it best not to alarm her any more than she was evident.

She stood quietly frozen in place. The basket she carried slipped from her hand and fell to the ground with a gentle thud. His ears pricked to catch the sound of her breathing, to find the fear he was sure would be present, but there was neither. A single apple rolled to Aidan's knee and he picked it up. He kept his focus on the fruit, blinking to quicken to the transition of his eyes to their natural color. A tangy, sweet residue lingered below his lip. He wiped his mouth with the back of his hand just as she decided to come to life.

"Oh, by the goddess almighty, what evil thing have ye done?" she asked. Her eyes searched his, yet she was not afraid. That alone intrigued him.

He stood calmly returning her sedate demeanor and turned the fragrant red fruit in his hand, acutely aware of how firm was the polished skin between his fingers. His gaze drifted from her bare feet upwards over the sheer white cotton of her linen tunic. She wore nothing beneath. He squeezed the apple, careful to release it before it exploded in his hand. "It's unfortunate that you came along when you did. In a few hours his body will be dust."

"Yer one of... them, then?" she asked, looking up at him. "One of the night folk?"

Her tongue had that familiar lilt that Aidan found titillating and he was curious to know what other skills it might possess. He shrugged. Having just satiated his appetite there was no threat of her becoming a meal. He licked his lips and eyed her voluptuous curves. Then again, she should run now since she'd sparked a carnal need far greater and there was danger that she'd wind up in his bed—and for a good long while if he had anything to say about it.

"You aren't afraid of me?" Aidan took a step toward her. His fingers curved around the apple, squeezing it gently as his gaze drifted to her ample cleavage.

Very nice.

Her gaze swept over him and then she quickly dropped on all fours, appearing, at least to his best judgement looking for something. He smiled and folded his arms over his chest, enjoying the view. Unless she had a sword, maybe a stake nearby, it didn't appear he was in imminent danger. Still, dead corpse notwithstanding, he supposed he appeared an imposing figure to her. At six-three, his mode of dress when traveling was black leather jeans, same color shirt and a sumptuous leather jacket given to him by a fellow lover of all things supernatural in return for his mortal life. He was happy to see Mr. Copperfield continuing to do well at the Grand. Aidan flicked his incisors and took a step closer to the woman still searching the ground. Her tenacious spirit amused him. Not once had she screamed—not even at the sight of him hovering over the dead body. It seemed she knew *what* he was and yet chose to remain.

Interesting.

"Stop, I say! Not another step closer, mind you. Ah, there 'tis." She grabbed for something behind her, scrambled to her feet, and with a fierce look of determination, shoved a long string of garlic in his face.

Aidan grimaced at the vegetable's annoying and pungent odor, reticent to tell her that his body had over the years built up an immunity to garlic. Her attempts were quaint, albeit old-fashioned.

"Dunna come any closer," she warned, shaking the garlic like a snake.

"Right." He frowned. "About *that*." Aidan scratched my chin, realizing that he hadn't shaved this morning in his haste to feed.

She shook it with persistence as though it might matter. Little wisps of garlic skin floated to the ground like snow. Ah, there it was. Her breathing grew rapid and he detected the fear growing inside her. Under normal circumstances, it would have fed his ego. He wanted more time with this woman—it was the first time he'd felt unguarded around a mortal. "I don't think I've ever met anyone like you."

"Then I'd just soon keep it that way, if it matters not to you." She held the garlic high in front of her and warned him off with a stern pointing of her finger.

"What if I said I wouldn't hurt you?"

She laughed and eyed him, nodding to the dead man on the ground. "Did you say that to him afore you bled him dry?"

"I admit that may taint things, but in truth, my word is my honor." He held out the apple to her. "And you can put that away, it does not have an effect on me."

Her storm-filled eyes flicked from the garlic strand back to him. "Yer word, then, that no harm shall come to me?"

There was a measure of fear in her eyes, but she was strong, this one. Her shoulders thrust back, chin held high, her focus squarely on him. If she'd had a bow tied around her, she couldn't have been a greater gift to his weary soul.

She took the apple and lowered the garlic. Her breasts rose and fell gently as she tried to control her fear.

"I will not harm you, I swear." Aidan lifted a hand to her cheek, soft as a flower petal it was. Her beautiful eyes—the color of a lush forest—drifted shut, her cheek pressed into his palm. He smiled at how easily she surrendered to his power. *I want you in my bed this night.*

"Aye, Milord, take me as you wish. I am yours," she spoke in her soft dreamlike state.

That was easy.

She gazed up at him and offered a sweet smile. He took it as her invitation and lowered his head to sample the mouth that had tempted him from the first moment he saw her.

She tipped her head, her gaze narrowing. "Do you think that yer charm is enough to sweep me off my feet, dark one?"

"Dark one?" Aidan scoffed rearing back to look at her. Though the title was indeed catchy, more important, he must be losing his animal magnetism. Damn, and he was so close to scoring.

"Do I look like the type to go to bed with the first man that comes along?" She fisted her hands on her lovely hips.

***

Aidan glanced over his shoulder at the chap on the ground and made a tsking sound. "I wouldn't dream of it, my heart."

She frowned and then looked him over, her gaze lingering in a couple of key spots along the way. "Humpf, my heart, you say. And why should I?"

He blinked. "Why should you come home with me, you mean?" Aidan answered her question with one of his own.

"Aye, give me one good reason, why I should agree to let you take me to yer bed. Ye haven't told me yer given name."

"Aidan," he responded quickly. Her banter was doing strange things to him, arousing him. It was a different style of foreplay, but he liked it. He grinned. "I can assure you that where I take you is beyond your wildest imagination."

She cocked her dark brow. "A braggart are ye now?"

Aidan splayed his hands. "Just stating the facts, ma'am."

She eyed him warily.

"Let's just say I'm a shrewd businessman, and I don't make promises I can't keep." He took her hand, letting his lips linger on her delicate skin. Aidan felt the rapid rush of her pulse, signaling her arousal. Oh yes, they would be good together, he was growing more and more convinced of it if the tightness in his jeans was any indication. "Just this once, and I promise you will not want to leave."

"My things." She eyed the spilled contents of her bag.

"You'll have no need for them where I'm taking you."

"What must I do?" Her eyes held his as he wrapped his arm around her waist.

He lowered his head and whispered. "Hang on."

Their affair lasted years. They'd spend the days together in the Penthouse hot tub and lounging by the fireside. She loved to read and he loved to doze off listening to her. Each night as the sun settled in the desert sky, they wandered the city, seeing the fountains, sampling black truffle soup at Savoy's, sharing spaghetti at Battista's Hole In the Wall, holding hands while strolling the Bellagio Gallery. He introduced to her to the many shows. Embracing the pulse that throbbed in the heart of the city and late into the shank of the evening, he'd take her to his bed, her passion-filled screams echoing in the dark. It was for Aidan the closest slice of heaven he would ever see. And as much as he begged, pleaded for her to become immortal, she would only give freely of her body, to the rest, she refused.

Then the day came that she asked him to take her home. She missed Britannia. She wanted to die in her homeland. It was the day his cold heart, froze solid.

***

Aidan was pulled from the depth of his reverie by the ringing of the phone. Who could be calling at this hour of the night? He could have easily let the answering machine pick it up, but few people had this number and curious, he picked it up, settling it casually on his ear. The moment he did, his senses came alive to the woman on the other end. His sensitive hearing picked up the anxiety in her breathing. He pushed aside the rush of need in his blood, blaming it on his previous thoughts. "Hello?"

"Is this a Mr. McGuire?"

Her voice, that tone—Aidan blinked, refocusing his efforts on the present. "It is, and who might this be?"

"My name is Lucynda Cavanaugh. Your name was given to me as a person who might be interested in the preservation of the historic library in town."

His flesh prickled. He was not half as interested in some old building or a million dusty books as he was knowing more about this woman. But if they came as a package, he was all ears. "I'm sorry, you said your name was?"

"Lucynda Cavanaugh," she responded rather succinctly, as if she hadn't the time to piss around.

The woman was on a mission. That was fine with him. In view of how his body reacted to her voice, it appeared he, too, had just started a mission of his own. In all of his days of wandering, there had only been one other woman he'd known by that name. It couldn't be coincidence.

"Your name, is that Gaelic, Ms. Cavanaugh?" Aidan asked. He turned to face the picture window that gave a view of the bustling nightlife below. Lights scattered across the desert, sparkling as though someone had tossed a sea of multi-colored gems across it. He felt his dead heart twitch. Could she be out there? Perhaps in some hotel room, seated on the edge of the bed? A delicious throbbing caused him to shift his stance, bringing his mind back from his torrid thoughts.

"Yes, I suppose it is, Mr. McGuire. Though I've never really looked into my heritage before."

He sensed the regret in her voice. He sensed everything about her, much to the discomfort in his jeans. That would teach him not to go commando. "What is it you want from me, Ms. Cavanaugh?" he asked, praying she would invite him to her room. He ran his tongue over his teeth, flicking the sharpened edges of his elongated incisors. Other parts of his body were responding with the same enthusiasm.

"I understand you possess an extensive collection of rare and classic books and we, that is I, was wondering if we might count on your support at a small gala fundraiser we're giving at the library in a few weeks."

He detected the gentle swallow that followed her query. Her anxiety fluttered over the wire. Could this be *his* Lucynda? Finally, after all these years? He'd attended enough past-life sessions to understand the possibility existed. Hell, he was a living example of it. But without aid of the curse. Was it possible? He fought the urge to delve into her subconscious and see for himself if she remembered him. "I don't know how you came by this number, but I don't usually appear socially, Ms. Cavanaugh."

"I apologize for the late call. I received a text from one of the library board members, though I've not met him personally... uh, a Mr. Bishop? He gave me your number stating you'd be very interested in our cause."

Aidan glanced back at the bar and saw a raised glass against the dark silhouette. *Thanks, Joey.* "Of course, I would be willing to make a sizable donation and please, no concerns about the hour, I'm a bit of a night-owl." He felt the pulse in her throat trip and he swallowed hard to tamp down his growing desire.

"That is most generous of you, Mr. McGuire. Do you believe then in the preservation of our past?"

The question came out of left field. He offered a quiet chuckle. "You've no idea, Ms. Cavanaugh, just how much."

"You're a very interesting man, Mr. McGuire," she said softly.

"How is that, Ms. Cavanaugh?" There was something very erotic in the formality of their words. Eerily familiar, of an era gone by where addressing a man or woman in such a way was commonplace. Yes, stealing kisses beneath a willow, while the lady addressed you by your proper name causes more than a man's blood to rise.

"So few here seem to know you well, and yet you are so generous in preserving what means most to them."

"I love old books, Ms. Cavanaugh. Is that so unusual?"

"So I understand. Based on your sizable contribution to the library of books on ancient Celtic lore and Gaelic legends, I assume you have a deep love for the old country."

The hairs on the back of Aidan's neck bristled. "For a woman who has not researched her lineage, you sound almost wistful when you mention the old country."

Her gentle laugh stroked his frustrated mind.

"I suppose it's one of those places one feels a kinship to, but for whatever reasons, you cannot get there. Have you ever felt that way, Mr. McGuire?"

"Many a time," he responded, his suspicions deepening that Lucynda's soul, was buried somewhere deep inside this woman. "Perhaps we should meet here at the Excelsior and discuss your plans for the library?"

"That sounds very nice, Mr. McGuire, but unfortunately our meeting will have to wait until the gala. I'm catching a flight tonight. I have a brother in London who is getting married."

"London?"

"Aye, London."

"Excuse me?" He gripped the receiver at the sound of the old world response. He stood a breath from transporting to her side.

"Forgive me. It's something that my Gran used to say. It slips out when I'm tired."

Aidan sucked in a deep breath, the muscle of his jaw ticking under the strain as he fought not to seduce her right then. It would be so easy. A simple, willful thought and he could be there, take the receiver from her hand, place it on the nightstand. He'd start first with the slow thrum at the base of her neck, just below her ear, still warm from the receiver. From there he'd peel away the blouse he was sure she wore under a business jacket—black, he guessed—with a pencil skirt that hugged her hips. He could almost hear the gentle rasp of the skirt sliding over her stockings at the insistence of his hands. And the sublime joy of finding old-fashioned black lace circling her thighs.

"Do you happen to be wearing black stockings, Ms. Cavanaugh?" he said softly, taking a precarious step in the direction of his thoughts.

There was a silence on the other end of the phone. He felt her pulse quicken, her body temperature rising steadily. *Damn.* Aidan steeled himself against the desire to work his mouth up those silky thighs and draw her stockings down with his teeth.

"Um, I think I should go, Mr. McGuire."

He detected her sudden hesitancy, realizing he'd gone too far. "Forgive me, Ms. Cavanaugh. I admit I am a pushover for a take-charge kind of woman."

She cleared her throat.

He imagined her, straightening her shoulders in a business-like resolve. He felt her backing away. "When will you be returning then, from London?" he asked, scolding himself for trekking too far into her psyche.

"Not until the night of the gala, I'm afraid."

"And do you have a date for that evening?" He didn't think before he asked.

"You've decided to come?" She did not mask her surprise.

"Only if you permit the Excelsior to host your gala. Then yes, I am yours, body and soul."

"You mean, heart and soul," she corrected picking up on the song reference.

"I mean, whatever parts appeal to you most," he replied.

"I don't know quite what to say, Mr. McGuire."

"It is simple. Say, yes, Ms. Cavanaugh. I am quite certain you will see that the Excelsior is the perfect venue and I your most perfect host."

She laughed softly and there was a lilt in her voice when she spoke, "Very well then. My staff will be in contact with you about the details and I guess I'll see you two weeks from tonight."

"The pleasure will be mine, Ms. Cavanaugh."

"Please call me, Lucynda," she offered quietly.

"If you call me Aidan," he responded.

"How will I know you?"

"You needn't worry, Lucynda. I am certain you will know when you see me."

The soft tinkle of the piano keys brought this head up as he ended the call. He'd had the baby grand brought up years ago, placing it in a corner of the suite, overlooking the city. "Hello Lee," he said, walking to the bar to pick up the scotch that had been left for him by his pal, Joey.

"Sounds like you managed to use your charm on that one, Aidan."

He smiled at his old friend. One of many who'd eventually made the thirteenth floor of the Excelsior their home. He didn't mind them dropping in unannounced. He was guilty of doing the same. Tonight was the eve of the feeding season and between the strange phone call and his growing hunger, he was restless. The strains of *I'll Be Seeing You*, floated in the air. Doubtful anyone on the floors below would think anything of it.

"This was one of my most requested favorites." The man smiled, his face lighting with an aura that once drew thousands of adoring fans.

"Just keep the music at a tolerable level, Lee. You know how the current manager gets when he has to explain the unexplainable to his guests. Aidan had an "arrangement" with the manager. He would deal with the living, Aidan, would handle the—no-longer-living.

"I promise to be a good boy." His nose wrinkled in impish delight, and as he waved his hand the tapers of the ornate candelabra ignited, offering an ethereal glow to the room. "That's better." Lee liked things to be esthetically pleasing to the eye.

Aidan picked up his crystal and pointed a finger at Lee. "You stop teasing Dean. You know how he gets."

Lee crossed his bejeweled hand over his heart and winked.

Aidan held the crystal, homed in on an era and found himself hurtled through space.

***

Aidan tiptoed over the bodies strewn across the smoke covered battlefield. His mission twofold. To feed and offer mercy. Upon his arrival through the cords of time, he'd followed the scent of blood, finding the wounded that had no hope to recover. It was his reasoning—as he drank freely, nourishing his body—that he was doing them a favor, putting them out of their agony. Tonight, he crouched, ankle deep in a rice paddy. Patches of long reeds swayed in the water, shielding him from view.

Remnant fires caused by mortar attacks burned bright in the distance. The occasional sound of machine guns erupting gave him pause during his feedings. In the distance, he heard the angry shouts of soldiers speaking in Vietnamese. In all the years, having seen so many wars firsthand, it never failed to puzzle him that mortals were far more capable of snatching more lives than were his people.

The moon shone through the smoky aftermath of mortar fire and he did not have to look at his hands to know they were covered in blood. He bent, swirling them in the rice paddy murky water and heard a faint sound.

"Help me," a raspy whisper came from the dense reeds to his right.

Aidan listened carefully and homed in the voice, cautious of those that may yet have life and mistake him for the enemy. A well-placed bayonet could cause more problems than he needed. He sloshed through the water and stumbled onto dry land.

He found a young man lying in a blind of reeds, the full moon illuminating his features. His face was covered in dirt and blood. Only his blue eyes shone in the surreal light. Aidan leaned down, his hunger for now appeased. "What can I do for you, boy?" he asked.

The young man struggled to breathe. Aidan saw the gash robbing the boy of his life's blood. He fought a primal urge to dip his head and appease himself. The boy, likely no more than twenty, if that, reached for his breast pocket with a trembling hand.

"I need you to give this to my wife. She's back in London, still." He coughed spewing up blood. "We've just had our first born... a boy."

He handed Aidan a photograph. Cautiously, Aidan accepted it and glanced down at it. He had to be careful of interaction of the dying unless he was sure they had no more time left on this earth.

"Send it back to her. It's her and my boy, Samuel. The address is on the back. Could you please write and tell her that my last thoughts were of her and Sam and that I love them both."

He grabbed Aidan's arm with amazing strength. "Please tell me that you'll do this, I beg you."

Aidan covered the boy's bloody hand and flipped over the picture, making sure the address was there as he'd said. "I can try," he said, not knowing how he'd manage the task, if by doing so he might change the course of things to come.

The wounded soldier coughed again, his hand reached wildly for Aidan. Then he lay still. Aidan brushed his fingers over the boy's eyes, closing them, then turned over the photo and read it by the light of the full moon.

"Hurry home, we love you. Lucynda and the other handsome Cavanaugh in my life, Samuel."

***

It was a week until the library fundraiser. Aidan had spent hours poring over his computer screen, searching ancestral links to every Cavanaugh from the mid-sixties to present day. What he found made his own existence pale in comparison. Samuel Cavanaugh had married a woman from Ireland and they lived in London for a time. They had three sons, one, a missionary to South Africa, who went missing and later was presumed dead. The second, a musician and who once taught at the University, the third traveled to the States to find his fame and fortune in the publishing business. Well known as both a writer and journalist, he married a young woman from Ireland he'd met while on a study abroad program through college.

In rapt fascination, Aidan followed the lineage, his gut alerting him to a truth that he barely could understand. He clicked the next link and there was, as clear of a confirmation that he could hope for. He smiled, easing back in his chair and read how the fates had shown him a path directly to her.

"Born on December twenty-first, in the year nineteen hundred and eighty-one." Aidan took a sip of his Loch Dhu, savoring the slow burn down his throat. He licked his lips, not wasting a drop of the charred perfection. "A girl—Lucynda Grace, born to Mr. Frederick S. and Anne Cavanaugh."

He looked at the photo that he'd taken the liberty of making a copy of before he'd found an envelope and slipped it into the Army mailbag being flown out that night. Aidan lifted his glass as he looked at the young woman and her smiling son. "Thank you, Samuel. Well done."

***

Crowds bothered him. But he'd drag himself down to a roomful of besotted, red-nosed library patrons for the sole chance that *this* Lucynda, was somehow *his* Lucynda. She did not know it yet, but a well-placed jog to that part of her psyche involving past-life, and he was positive she'd remember. Aidan adjusted his tie, surprised by his nervousness. "One before I go downstairs." He took a seat at the luxurious bar, well-stocked as always for him and a few of his best friends.

"As you like, sir," the clipped voice of the man behind the bar stated. "Don't mind of I join you. It appears to be an auspicious occasion." He picked a martini—very dry.

Aidan lifted the centuries-old scotch and drained it. He glanced at his friend. "I'm nuts, Dean? To think this might be her?"

Dark eyes, coupled by a dimpled smile that had probably gotten him far with the ladies eyed him. "If she's *the one*, then you go for broke. You know what I say, son. Everybody loves somebody— sometime." He crooned the rest of the sentence in his rich baritone.

"The man has got a point, Aidan. I mean, when it comes to the opposite sex, you gotta do-be-do what you do best, bro." Seated at the end of the bar, Frank raised his glass. "Hey, anyone seen Smokey?"

"Candy man has arrived, gentlemen. Just caught a show over at the old haunt—well, where it used to be. Man, that Venetian is some pretty classy digs. You know what I mean?" He swaggered up to the bar and removed his shades as he looked around. "I see the Clan is almost here. The best of them at any rate." He brushed the lapel of his steel grey silk suit. "Can you dig it, babies?"

"Guys, I'm going to need all of you to channel your energies tonight." Aidan glanced from one to the other of the A-listers standing around him. Spirits this bright in the Vegas strip could never die. Their power beats in brilliant syncopation in the heart of the city and in no place stronger than at the Excelsior. A shrewd businessman and immortal, Louis "The Lip" LaFica had a purpose when he built the Excelsior in the shadow of the Sands. Years later, in 1996, when it was demolished, one after another drifted to the Excelsior where the current owner, Aidan McGuire, welcomed them with open arms. Present-day guests at the Excelsior claim to they've seen the ghosts of the Rat Pack in shadowed corridors, or just off-stage in the ballroom. Then again, the booze flows freely here in Sin City, where anything is possible and *most* of what happens here, stays here.

"Go get her, champ. We'll be watching from the cheap seats." Frank swirled his drink in his glass.

Aidan lifted another scotch that had appeared in front of him. He smiled at Dean, who merely nodded. "You guys are the best friends a guy could ever have." It was the scotch and his nerves making him sound mushy.

"Son." Dean leaned across the bar. "We're the *only* friends you got."

Leave it to friends to set things straight. Aidan finished his drink. "Fair enough." He stood, shook down his tuxedo sleeves. "Man-bun look okay?" He checked their faces.

"Man-bun." Sammy shook his head. "Reminds me of the sixties."

Aidan bypassed checking in the mirror. He knew he looked good. He hoped Lucynda would feel the same. "Later, gentleman... oh, and if there's a sock on the doorknob, I trust you'll stay out tonight." He closed the door to an array of whistles and catcalls.

He could easily have appeared in the third floor ballroom. But the last time he'd transported without checking first, he wound up in the ladies' restroom, unaware of the changes that had been made on that floor. Instead, he chose to blend in and take the elevator. A bevy of scents assaulted him as he smiled and nodded, wedging himself among the humans stuffed like a snack-pack in the elevator. He was grateful he'd thought to feed before the gala as he stepped off the crowded elevator and into a sea of black ties and gowns. He glanced around with a pleased smile and hoped they would stay and partake of the Excelsior's casino later on. He wove through the sea of humanity to the ballroom entrance and stood for a moment, pleased with how his suggestions had been brought to life. Old World opulence was everywhere, from the stained glass hangings to the massive fountain at the center of the room. Baskets of fresh lavender graced every table centerpiece, their fragrant scent creating a calming nostalgia to the setting. It was a Celtic Lords delight and he hoped it would speak to the heart of Lucynda.

Aidan drew in a sharp breath as if a woman had touched him intimately. His gaze shot to the double-wide entrance of the room. There she stood—as beautiful and fresh as the last time he'd seen her. His body's response was powerful and he turned to a nearby bartender and requested a glass of his private stock.

"Your Loch Dhu, Mr. McGuire," the man stated, handing him a glass. He swallowed it in one gulp as he watched her walk toward him.

Aidan blinked and stood looking into the eyes of the woman who'd plagued his immortal existence.

"I'm glad to see you found a reason to join the land of the living, Mr. McGuire."

He had to steel himself from taking her into his arms and kissing her senseless. "Miss Cavanaugh, I presume?" He offered his hand and she took it as he placed a kiss on her delicate fingers. The scent was just as he remembered. *Unforgettable.*

"Lucynda Cavanaugh," she offered drawing her hand away. She gave him a curious look.

"A beautiful name for a beautiful lady," he responded, offering a brief courteous bow. "Is that Irish or Scottish?"

Her eyes, a lush green with gold and brown flecks, sparked with interest and it hit Aidan in the solar plexus. "Irish, I think." She eyed him, then glanced around the room. "You are a lover of old things, then, Mr. McGuire?" she asked

He grinned. "Indeed, Ms. Cavanaugh, you might say that I am both a connoisseur of old things and a lover as well." Her dark hair sprouted corkscrew tendrils that lay against her porcelain neck. He imagined his mouth nibbling there, his teeth scraping the scent from her skin.

Her sumptuous mouth dropped slightly, recovering with a quick smile. "They told me you were blunt."

"I don't believe in wasting time, Ms. Cavanaugh. For the living, it is far too precious to fill with wasted jargon, dribbled words that but delay the inevitable."

Her eyes blinked as if digesting his sexual magic, like incense wafting from his aura to hers.

"You don't believe in the whole getting to know someone first idea?"

"There are some things that two people know without saying a word, Ms. Cavanaugh."

She drew her hand to the base of her throat, her eyes, hesitant to look at him.

"Forgive me if my manner is out-of-line. It is rare to find beauty and intelligence in one tantalizing package." He made no pretense of letting her see how he assessed her. "A most tantalizing package," he repeated, demanding mentally that she look at him. There was no doubt in his mind that before the night was through, she would be his and to his liking, this time it would be for all eternity.

She swallowed and he could almost taste her lips. "May I get you a drink?" he asked.

"Riesling," she answered.

Aidan put in her order and turned to find her staring at him. He felt confident that it wasn't the suit she was looking at. He gave her an easy smile, one that you'd give your lover across the room. One that held promise that tonight was going to be magical. He handed the drink to her. "Riesling for the lady."

"Thank you, Mr. McGuire." She studied him and shook her head with a smile.

"What is it?" he asked.

"It's strange, but we've never met before, have we?"

Aidan battled with projecting to her mind the last night they spent as one. Limbs entwined in a tangle of sheets, her body glistening in the candlelight, the grip of her fingers on his forearms as she arched her back towards him. Aidan shoved his thoughts back to the present and noted the glazed look in Lucynda's eyes—definitely arousal. He forced himself to think of other things. It would not do to have her unravel here in the midst of the charity crowd, better to wait in private. "Would you care to dance?" he asked, lifting the glass from her hand before she answered.

"Oh, well, I suppose… "

He placed his hand on the small of her back and led her to the small dance floor, a fake parquet, that they'd placed at the edge of the room. He took her in his arms, remembering how they once danced together at the old tavern. Then, it had been a raucous jig, tonight, the song was designed just for her—*Unforgettable*.

Her body swayed with his and if she was uncomfortable with how tightly he held her, she didn't comment. Aidan, breathed in the scent of her hair, her skin, a blend of exotic scents—jasmine, lavender and ylang ylang. It would be easy to dance her into the shadows and by the mere thought of it, transport her back to his bed where he would enjoy finding out how long that zipper was on the back of her low-cut gown.

"The wine must be doing strange things, Mr. McGuire," she said. "I'm feeling a bit shaky. Do you mind if I sit down?"

"Of course. Perhaps outside on the balcony, where you can get some fresh air?"

She nodded and he was pleased when she curled her arm through his without a word and followed him outside.

The moon, high in the clear night sky, was at three-quarters and a gentle cool breeze blew across the desert, lending a near perfect ambiance to Aidan's plans.

He ushered her to a stone bench and sat beside her and stared up at the star-sprinkled sky. He would let her catch her breath before he took it away from her a second time.

"I don't know what happened," she said, her gaze flickering to his. "I hardly know you and yet I feel as though I've known you forever."

He studied her beautiful eyes and then dared to brush his knuckle beneath her chin, tilting it toward him. "Funny that you should say that. I feel exactly the same."

"Is that odd?" she asked, not taking her eyes from his.

"I prefer to think of it as fate, Lucynda." He gazed deep into her soul. "I don't want you to be frightened, but I am desperate to kiss you."

"Why would that frighten me?" she asked softly.

Already her mind was fertile to the truth. "You will understand soon and with this knowledge will come a choice that you must make." He leaned closer, his mouth barely brushing hers, drinking in her essence, feeling her lifeblood heating with arousal.

The instant his mouth touched hers, the images of their first night together exploded with fury in his mind. Clothes strewn in a path to his bed, she had not asked then, where they were. The passion between them so strong that all else melted away. He'd held back that night from making her immortal. He'd wanted her to come willingly. To accept freely his eternal worship of her body and soul. Long after they'd made love several times, he'd waited, watching the firelight shimmering on her body, waiting for the one word from her that would change his immortal hell to heavenly salvation.

***

Aidan nipped at Lucynda's lip and watched the flutter of her eyelashes as the heated images of love and passion seeped into her subconscious. "I'm waiting still for your answer, my love," he whispered, slanting his mouth over hers again. He purposely withdrew from her when she sought to deepen the kiss. It was then he knew she stood on the verge of understanding how she'd come to be in his arms.

His gut clenched when a soft cry came from her throat. "I've waited so long... so long to find you." Aidan pressed his forehead to hers, the need in his loins growing desperate. He needed an answer soon. "Please, Lucynda, do not make me suffer any longer." Aidan swore if he had a heart, it was aching. Everything ached.

Lucynda lifted her gaze to his and her lips moved. Bending closer, he looked into her eyes and saw what played in her mind. There was the image of the two of them stretched out on the bed. He was tracing the delicate curve of her neck... waiting for an answer.

"Aidan, at last," his Celtic lover whispered.

The soft sound of her voice, pulled Aidan back to the present. He searched her face. "Are you sure, Lucynda?" he asked.

"Yes, my love. I remember." she said quietly. "I've been waiting… so long."

Heat surged through his blood and he smiled, his incisors lengthening. He targeted the spot on her neck, where her life-pulse throbbed with need. "Be sure," he gave her one final chance to refuse.

She tilted her head, offering her slender neck. "Take me, my love."

Aidan pressed his lips to her throat, his teeth sinking into her buttery-soft flesh. He seduced her mentally showing her each and every possible way he planned to worship her for all time.

Her body trembled and he tightened his embrace, drinking deeply as she tumbled over the edge with a soft sigh, and he right along with her. For a moment, she lay still in his arms. He held her waiting, until at last her eyelids fluttered, and she looked up at him in dreamlike wonder.

"Aidan?"

"Aye, my love. How do you feel?"

She straightened, adjusted her gown, and then smiled. "I'm oddly hungry, ravenous actually." She touched his cheek. "But happier than I've been in years."

"I promise to take care of that hunger soon, my darling. But first, I want to finish our dance."

As though on cue, the band started playing one of his Sinatra favorites—one of many. He pulled Lucynda into his arms, pressed his cheek to hers, and saluted the row of silhouettes seated like polished gargoyles along the stone wall of the balcony.

Frank's signature voice, wrapped in the Vegas moonlight sang along with the band, never skipping a beat as it carried softly on the night breeze. *"Never ever change, keep that breathless charm, won't you please arrange it, cause I love you, and the way you look tonight."*

4

GANGSTER LOVE AFFAIR

Hailey J. Bissell

"Where is she, Finn?" The eerily calm, deep voice came from the dark corner of an old dilapidated room. A middle-aged man slumped in a chair in the other corner. His hands and feet were bound tightly to the chair by thick, coarse rope. A light swung from the ceiling above him. Blood dribbled from his mouth onto the floor. He chuckled. He had been hit before. The more it happened, the funnier it became.

"I had a feeling you'd come and join the party, Johnny Boy." Finn lifted his head. Blood ran down from a deep cut on his forehead. His eyes, although black and swollen, seemed delighted with the sound of a familiar voice, or maybe it was the shark-like grin plastered on his face that gave it away. "I've been waiting, Johnny Boy, while your kids here have been trying to show me a good time. Don't be too hard on them, they really did try." He licked his lips and grinned again. Two men stood on both sides of Finn. They towered over him. Thick muscled arms hung motionless at their sides, knuckles bloodied. Both wore black pinstriped suits, ties, and fedora hats that were speckled with Finn's blood. Their facial expressions never changed. They stared into the voice's dark corner and nodded, not moving any other muscles.

"Where is she, Finn?" the voice repeated the question in the same tone.

Finn's smile grew harder. "Come on now, Johnny Boy. You and I both know the game too well," Finn said with slight offense. "Do you remember that old saying? Time is our best friend, and our worst enemy?" Finn asked.

There was a moment of pause between the two until Johnny stepped into the light. He was in his late twenties and had short brown hair, tall and handsome features with a chiseled physique. He was dressed to the nines in a sleek, sexy tux. A single purple flower slumped from his lapel. His face showed no emotion, but his cold green eyes told all. They were laced with red lines, and dark bags hung below them. Sleep had always come easy to Johnny. Having an entire city as your "prey" ground gave you that unbreakable confidence. The problem with a "prey" ground is there's always someone who thinks they're bigger, badder, and ready to make it their own.

"Then let's talk business, Finn. Tell me where the girl is, and I make your death less painful." His voice kept the same, calm tone.

Finn's bloody grin returned. "That a boy. See, it's all about negotiations. I knew I taught you better," Finn said. He spat blood onto the floor and leaned back in his chair. "You know how it works. I give you something, you give me something. Deal?"

"Deal," Johnny said.

"Tell the kids here to grab my jacket. They let me take it off before the party started. It's my favorite," Finn said as he chortled.

Johnny looked at his watch and rubbed his eyes. He snapped his fingers. A minute later, a short, stocky man in the same outfit as the big goons came out with a black- and blue-striped jacket. There was a long scar across his right eye. He handed the jacket to Johnny.

"Thank you, Frankie," Johnny said.

Frankie nodded and went back into the dark corner. Finn eyed Johnny and shook his head in disapproval.

"'Thank you?' Boy, she really did a number on ya, kid. If your father was still alive, you'd be in my chair," Frankie said.

Johnny ignored the comment and searched Finn's jacket pocket. He found Finn's familiar red handkerchief. As he unfolded it, he discovered a pink pearl earring inside. Johnny had been in these situations before, probably a hundred times. Not once did he ever hold his breath in anticipation. Not even when his arch-nemesis took his best friend and sent his finger with the ring he had given him for his birthday as proof of his abduction. He did what he normally did: beat the piss out of the informant until he got what he wanted. Johnny was always business, no matter who, no matter what. There was no time or room for anyone to be anything else. People were always expendable. Pawns in a never-ending game.

But this time, all Johnny could see was the night he had given them to her. The feel of her soft, supple skin in his fingertips as he put them on her ears. He could hear the sound of excitement in her voice. She had inherited a pair from her mother, who was murdered when she was thirteen. They meant the world to her, but had been stolen. Johnny wanted to give her everything her heart desired. He wanted to make up for all the pain from her past. The earrings were a sign of his promise to always protect her. He remembered her gorgeous blue eyes that sparkled as she looked at the present. Those eyes were as blue as the ocean on a tropical paradise. Johnny knew that when you looked into someone's eyes, you saw their soul. There were very few souls that Johnny allowed himself to see. If it had a soul, it was no longer a game piece. That is until he met her. He looked at her soul every chance he got. That night was the first night he truly allowed himself to see her for who she was. He fell in love with her. The only woman he ever loved. His mother had died in childbirth, so he never had a memory of her to love, only the stories his father told him. But he had Isabella.

***

One look at her earring and he was back a month earlier, when Isabella walked into the Excelsior for the first time. Isabella's long black hair flowed in ringlets around her shoulders, and a purple flower was held in place with a bobby pin. Three giant men loomed behind her. She walked up to the front desk and asked to speak with Johnny Boy.

"I'm here to see Mr. LaFica," Isabella said.

The young man behind the desk eyed her suspiciously. "I'm sorry, ma'am, he does not entertain visitors. Perhaps you could catch him in the club tonight," he said.

"Please tell him I have a message from The Cigar," Isabella said with a sultry Italian accent, "I promise, if he says personally that he doesn't want to speak with me, I will go." She leaned over the counter and stared into his eyes with a sweet smile of promise and tease.

He smiled back and fumbled to pick up the phone to make a call. He relayed the message nonchalantly. His eyes widened. Before he could say anything, the phone went dead. He put the phone back on the hook quickly. Isabella chuckled.

"I'm sorry for the confusion, Miss Carmine. An escort will take you to Mr. LaFica's office in just a moment," the young man said.

"Thank you," she said with a smirk.

A minute later, Frankie walked up to her side. He was dressed in his usual suit and tie.

"Miss Carmine, lovely to see you. Please, allow me to take you up to Johnny's office," Frankie said cordially. He looked at the three men taking a step to follow him.

"I'm sorry for the inconvenience, but he will only see you. No one else," he said. Before they could speak a word, Isabella held out her hand.

"Of course Mr. uh, I'm sorry I didn't catch your name," she said calmly. She had been raised to know power. She spoke and walked with confidence, not just from the authority she was under, but from fully being aware of her feminine charm and lure.

"'Frankie' is just fine," he smiled.

She turned to her bodyguards. "I'll be back in just a moment. Do not over extend our welcome, gentlemen."

"We will be waiting here for you. Do not take long, Miss Carmine. We must not keep your father waiting," one of the men said.

They turned and stood by the desk. Frankie tilted his head to them and allowed Isabella to hook on to his arm. The men watched as he led her to the elevators.

Johnny's office was very elegant, as far as offices went. The wood was beautiful, dark mahogany with gold trim. Everything had its place and was put there with precision and purpose, all except his Monets. He had always said the paintings helped him to escape from reality. Johnny Boy was sitting at his desk on a phone call. Johnny was always taught to dress out of respect for you and your business. He almost never saw his father in anything but a suit, which he wore to carry on the tradition. He finished his phone call as Frankie and Isabella entered the room.

Johnny saw only her as they walked in. She was the most beautiful woman he had ever seen. He remembered never wanting her to leave his sight. Every curve had the purpose of driving him to the brink of destruction. He thanked God in his mind for making something so perfect.

"Hello, Mr. LaFica. My name is Isabella. My father asked that I come to see you. Do you have a package for me?" she asked with confidence. Most women were quite nervous when they first met him.

He was a very handsome man and one of the most powerful men in the state. She had looked him straight in the eyes. No one ever did that.

"I was told your father would be meeting me. Does he always send a woman to do his bidding?" he asked coolly.

"Only when he knows a woman can do much better than a man ever could, Mr. LaFica," she said.

Frankie stifled a laugh. Johnny gritted his teeth but did not let it show.

"Very well, Miss Carmine," he started.

She interrupted, "'Isabella' would be fine, actually."

"Isabella, your father needed to provide me with my request first, and then you can go on your way," he said with a touch of frustration.

She reached into her purse and pulled out an envelope. "My apologies. This is for you," She handed him the envelope. His hand touched hers ever so slightly as he took it from her hand. He had wanted to grab her hand and pull her body into his and never let go. It scared him that around her he had trouble controlling his urges and emotions. He wanted all of her. Turning around, Johnny shook his head. He opened the envelope and viewed the contents.

"Mr. LaFica..." she interrupted his concentration.

"Frankie will take you downstairs. There will be a package waiting with your guards," he said.

He motioned to Frankie. Frankie nodded and offered Isabella his arm.

"Thank you, Mr. Lafica. I'm sure my father will be calling on you once he receives the package," she said. She smiled at him and turned to walk away.

"Um, Isabella, I'd like you to see my club tonight, if you have time," he said quickly.

Frankie looked at him, confused. Isabella smiled.

"Perhaps another time, Mr. LaFica. I shall be spending the evening with my father and Dominick Crillo. Thank you for your invitation," she said with a courteous smile.

"Very well, Miss Carmine, goodbye until we meet again," he said.

She smiled as though she knew something Johnny didn't. His gaze was set in stone.

"Goodbye, Mr. LaFica," she said with a velvet voice.

Johnny's stare followed her until the elevator doors shut. He picked up the phone and dialed with purpose.

"Hey, little Mo, its Johnny Boy. I need to speak with Cigar," he said.

That night Johnny waited for her at the club. It was a swanky nightclub with a live jazz band playing every brass instrument ever known. A gorgeous blond-haired flapper girl sang to all the men in the crowd. If she didn't entice them with her voice, she had the body of a goddess to finish the job. Tables and chairs crowded the floor. Men and women twirled and jived their way on the dance floor. Waiters served the Devil's nectar on trays. To the far right was a more private room for gaming. The joint was packed with politicians and mobsters alike. Anyone who was anyone in Las Vegas was there, and only the big boys with fat wallets were allowed in the gamblers hall. Johnny's private box overlooked the entire club. He sat in his usual chair. Frankie entered through the hidden side door holding a glass of water with lime.

"Has Lucky's luck run out yet?" Johnny asked Frankie with sarcasm.

Frankie smiled. "Not yet. Apparently poison is a long-lost tradition. The only time Lucky gets around the bend is when he eats his own food. Can't blame him, though. Victor put Tabasco sauce in his drink before, and Ronnie put laxative in his pudding. He was on the crapper for days," he said through laughter.

Johnny grinned. "So that's why he had been looking thin. Is everything set for tonight?" he asked.

"Copacetic, Boss," Frankie said.

Johnny was always back to business. His face never showed emotion from his normal calm demeanor. That was until Isabella walked into the club. Color began to creep up his face and his breath caught in his throat. Frankie chuckled and shook his head. Johnny never noticed. All he saw was her. Isabella had her hair pinned up in an elegant messy bun. Strands fell down her face. Her luscious lips were as red as a fire truck. Her dress matched them. It clung to every curve and flowed down to the floor. A slit bared her right leg up to her thigh as her heels wrapped seamlessly over her ankles. She was a fearsome thing to behold in Johnny's mind.

Isabella was being escorted by her father, Vinnie "The Cigar" Carmine. He was a man in his fifties, white hair, and eyes the color of dollar bills. His posture alone commanded respect. Close to Isabella's right side was Dominick "The Hammer" Crillo. He was as tall as a building and large as one to boot. Dominick was from Russia. Everyone knew once they heard his thick Russian accent. When his family came to the States, they changed their last name to Crillo. His father told him it was something that would help them to have a fresh start. He found out the hard way. They had come to hide from some big bad Russian mobster his father owed more than money to. Eventually they were found. His father and mother were killed in front of him when he was thirteen. The cops got there before they could kill him. That was the day he vowed vengeance. Once he killed the men responsible though, he never lost the bloodlust for power or rage. Everyone knew he was crazy. Most feared him. Johnny, however, accepted his challenge as foreplay. And then there was Finn next to Dominick. The same shark-like grin crossed his face. Finn looked up at Johnny and winked. Johnny clenched the railing.

Frankie nodded to Johnny and walked out of the room. He stared at the game ahead of him.

"Time to play," he said to himself.

A few minutes later, Frankie led Johnny's guests into his den. Dominick walked in first. He stood as stiff as a board and he walked with a sense of unrelenting arrogance. He smirked as he held out his hand for Johnny to shake. Johnny kept his cool demeanor. He liked having his enemies as close as possible.

"Why, Johnny, it's been too long," Dominick said.

Johnny shook his hand firmly.

"Mr. Crillo, I'm glad you accepted my invitation. Please have a seat." Johnny gestured to one of the chairs. "Would you like a Moscow Mule?" Johnny asked with a polite smile.

Dominick laughed. "Still keeping tabs on me I see, Johnny Boy. Thank you, but I do not wish to drink in front of the lady. She does not care for such libations," he answered.

"What is it that I do not care for, Mr. Crillo?" Isabella asked as her father escorted her to the table.

"Just your distaste for libations, my bella," he answered.

Isabella raised one eyebrow in disapproval. "I believe it makes foolish children out of men and women, Mr. Crillo. It also frees you to make choices that would make your life a living hell, isn't that right, Daddy?" She smiled.

"Fiery just like her mother," Vinnie said.

Dominick just smiled a very toothy grin. Johnny could not take his eyes off her. He stiffened ever so slightly. Dominick held his hand for her to grab as he led Isabella to her seat. Isabella noticed Johnny's posture and quirked her mouth a bit. Johnny quickly changed his attention to Vinnie and shook his hand.

"Mr. Carmine, it is always a pleasure. Thank you for breaking your dinner plans for the evening," Johnny said.

"Oh nothing earth-shattering, Johnny Boy," Vinnie said.

Everyone took a seat at the table. The waiter carried a tray of waters for all but Vinnie. He placed a scotch on the rocks in front of him and Vinnie slid a twenty-dollar bill into his other hand. Isabella looked at him disapprovingly.

"I will drink what I please, Isabella," Vinnie replied as he took another sip.

"So, Johnny, word is going round that you have a new business opportunity that will be worth my while," Dominick said. It was more of a statement than a question. Johnny knew he had spies all around and that his gang was getting larger each day.

"Yes, which is why I invited you all here tonight. To get down to the point, I know how big the drug scene is starting to become. I think we have an opportunity to get in the action and make a monopoly here. One who shall never be named can get us product relatively cheap. We triple our prices and make a small fortune. Maybe even throw some freebies to our whales, help them feel charitable with their chips," Johnny said.

Dominick laughed. "How do you expect to circulate it without getting caught? There are more coppers in town now that the Excelsior is here."

"Most are easily bought. Besides, I've made friendly with well-to-do politicians. I also plan on making more than one Excelsior. My father was right to have faith in the business Las Vegas brings. Ask Finn," Johnny said with a laugh.

"How will we bring the cargo to Las Vegas?" Vinnie asked. He signaled the bartender for another cocktail.

"It will be packed along with supplies for the hotel. As well as in the building materials for my next one," Johnny said. He looked at Isabella. She had been talking with Frankie, trying to ignore the conversation. Occasionally she would glance at Johnny with an almost sadness, yet her mouth held a smile like it normally did.

"Speaking of hotels, if this is to be a partnership, then I want control of one. I think it only fair to have power divided between all of us," Dominick said.

"That is not on the table, Mr. Crillo. My father built this town by himself. I intend to keep it that way," Johnny fired back.

"Yes and look where he ended up. Six feet under and nothing to show for himself," Dominick responded with amusement.

Johnny held back a growl deep in his chest. He smiled at Dominick.

"Mr. Crillo, your manners are quite poor this evening to our host. Please, Johnny, may we get back to business?" Vinnie said.

Isabella turned to Dominick as if to voice her opinion; however, Vinnie shook his head no. She bit her lower lip and said nothing. Dominick leaned closer to Isabella and left his hand on her thigh. Johnny saw red. He sipped at his water, trying to get his temper under control again.

"Johnny, you wanted to show me your nightclub, did you not?" Isabella asked Johnny.

"Yes, I believe I did," Johnny said. He stood up and held out his hand. Isabella gladly took it and stood by his side. Dominick gritted his teeth.

"You promised me a dance this evening, my darling," Dominick warned.

"Yes, Mr. Crillo; however, I made our host a promise first," Isabella retorted. She grabbed Johnny's arm and followed him into the elevator.

Dominick turned to face Vinnie with rage.

"You said she was mine," Dominick shouted to Vinnie.

"You know she will be yours," Vinnie replied, unmoved.

"Then why do you allow her to do as she pleases? She must obey—" Before Dominick could finish, Vinnie interrupted him.

"You know she is not a dog. My daughter is strong-willed like her mother. I may be able to force her to accept your proposal, but to earn her love and respect is entirely unto you," Vinnie said with authority and wisdom.

"Let me make this very clear to you, old man. Your debt to me grows deeper and deeper with each day. Should my engagement to Isabella not go as promised, then all you have belongs to me. Trust me, your daughter will be mine no matter what," Dominick hissed with promise.

He turned quickly to watch out the balcony.

Johnny had shown Isabella the bar, as well as the bartenders and waiters. Johnny had always tried to be cordial to his employees. He watched as she laughed with people in his club. The band began to play the tango.

He leaned over and whispered into her ear, "Isabella, will you dance with me?"

Isabella looked up at Dominick. He was staring at the two of them like a hawk, waiting for her next decision. Isabella looked at Dominick's eyes for a moment. Johnny could see the fight Isabella had in her mind. Everyone knew Dominick was a monster. Even though her father owed a terrible debt to Dominick, Johnny wanted her to know that he would take care of her. She looked back at Johnny and nodded.

Johnny took her by the waist and led her to the dance floor. He pulled her tightly against his body and began the dance. She followed every step he led and added a few bits of flare. Johnny's eyes widened when she did. Their bodies were one. He loved the way her skin felt against his. As they danced, all his problems were in the sea of forgetfulness. They were the only ones in the world at that moment in time: each move sensual, vigorous, and spontaneous. Sweat trickled down his neck and his breathing grew more rapid. To him it was like making love on the dance floor. He didn't even notice that the song had changed until Frankie came to Johnny with urgency. Johnny was holding Isabella in a dip as Frankie tapped on his shoulder.

"I'm sorry, Boss, but Vinnie needs to see you now. There was an altercation between him and Dominick," Frankie said.

Isabella's eyes grew wide as Johnny tilted her back up. He straightened his jacket and they followed Frankie to his balcony.

Vinnie was being held in a chair with a large gash on his shoulder. Blood dripped down onto his torn coat sleeve. Isabella rushed to his side and held his face.

"Daddy, I'm so sorry. I should have just stayed," Isabella said as a tear slid down her cheek.

Vinnie smiled at her. "Sweetheart, I'm all right. It's just one scratch. You should see the one I gave him. There will be a nice large scar across his face for the rest of his life. I am the one who got us in this mess. It is I who should be saying sorry," Vinnie said. Isabella hugged him fiercely.

Johnny looked at Vinnie's arm and motioned to the bartender for another drink. It would need stitches.

"Frankie, have you called Doc yet?" Johnny asked.

"Yes, Boss, he is almost here," Frankie replied.

"I think it's time we make the call Mr. Carmine. Dominick is planning something big, and after tonight he will think of nothing else. Vengeance will consume him again, and I'm afraid he's not alone," Johnny said calmly.

"What do you know?" Vinnie asked.

Frankie handed Johnny an envelope. Johnny pulled out pictures of different mobsters meeting with Dominick. He laid them around the table in front of Vinnie.

"As you know, my boys have been following him for months. I have a rat on the inside that keeps me updated. Dominick has been bringing different gangs into Vegas for weeks with the promise of fortune and fame. The package you intercepted from his men contained the original blueprints for the Excelsior. They are trying to find a way in. My father was a brilliant man, though, and had many different blue prints made," Johnny explained.

"One of your father's many secrets," Vinnie snorted.

"We need to begin preparations, Vinnie," Johnny said.

Isabella stood up and looked at them. "My instincts say to run, hide, and be gone from this place for good and never look back," she said.

"I am not in a position to leave, Isabella. This is my home and no one will take it from me. This hotel is the only thing left of my father. He put everything he had into it. I refuse to give it up so easily," Johnny said with tension in his voice.

Isabella stared at him and straightened up. "No, Johnny, your father put everything he had into you, not into something here one day and gone the next. I will do whatever it takes to make my family safe, and if that means we must trust you to do so, then you have it. As long as you do one thing, promise me that we will be safe," she said with total resolve.

"I promise," he said.

***

A large hand with a missing finger grabbed his shoulder and brought him out of his reverie. Johnny shook his head and gritted his teeth. Frankie whispered in his ear, took the jacket, and left. Johnny closed the handkerchief tightly in his hand.

"Where is she, Finn," Johnny asked coldly.

"Take, take, take. That wasn't our deal. Nor hers as you are well aware of, Johnny," Finn said. He sat back in the chair as best he could. A small sense of discomfort came from his eyes as he moved. His ribs were broken in a few places. He knew that sort of break well enough.

"What does he want, Finn?" Johnny asked.

"The Excelsior, of course." Finn smirked. "You give Dominick the Excelsior, and she walks free. It's only fair. He takes your love, just as you took his," Finn said.

"No deal. You know you are going to hell for asking me that, Finn. That hotel meant a lot to you too when my father was alive," Johnny spat.

"You know time is wasting, Johnny boy. If you refuse his offer, then they kill her. And trust me, it won't be quick," Finn said as he shook his head.

Johnny ran up to him and cracked his jaw with a hard punch. It knocked the chair onto the floor. Finn made a gurgling sound. It had been so long since Johnny had hit someone. He had enough people under him now who took care of that aspect for him. His goons tried to pick up Finn, but Johnny waved them off. He knelt down by Finn and pulled him up by the hair, fists ready to give blows. He looked at Finn's mangled face and dropped him.

"Why? Why, Finn? You are family. Why would you do it? He was your best friend. You both were like brothers, and you my mentor, my uncle. You kill your best friend, and then you help the enemy steal my love on the night I was proposing to her! Why? Why, Finn?" Johnny screamed with tears in his eyes.

"Things aren't always as they seem, kid," he wheezed.

Johnny swung his fist again, this time in Finn's gut. Finn cried out in pain and vomited. Frankie grabbed Johnny and pulled him away from Finn.

"They... have... her in the Excelsior," Finn gasped.

Johnny got back up on his feet and got close to Finn.

"What?" Johnny asked.

"Your girl, they have her at the Excelsior, Presidential Suite," Finn gasped again. "Don't ever say I didn't give you nothing," he said through shortened breaths. He smiled faintly and closed his eyes.

Johnny looked at his mentor while Frankie pulled him up onto his feet again.

"Boss, we need to move! The boys will handle the body!" Frankie said hurriedly.

The two big goons picked up Finn's body as Frankie drug Johnny out of the room.

The boys made it to the Excelsior in record time. They saw Dominick's men at the front entrance. Men and women dressed in their finest were walking into the hotel for the annual ball. They kept the car far enough from view.

"Hey, Boss, the boys say they have their men surrounding the hotel. How are we going to get in?" Frankie asked Johnny.

"The only way there is. Take us back behind that building to your far left," Johnny said as he pointed to some buildings across the street, a ways down from the hotel. His hair had been combed back, and he allowed his usual calm demeanor back onto the surface.

The cars pulled around the back entrance to a brick building. Everyone got out and collected near the back, metal doors. Johnny pulled the key out of his pocket and unlocked them. Everyone filed inside. The building was a warehouse. Crates upon crates were neatly piled high throughout the entire building. Johnny led his gang into the small office in the corner of the building. The office was furnished with an old wooden desk, one filing cabinet, and two chairs.

"We need to move the desk," Johnny said.

Four men quickly moved the desk with ease, revealing a large, metal trapdoor with a combination lock in the middle. Johnny moved the dial to the correct numbers until a loud clicking noise broke the silence of concentration. He pulled the trapdoor open. A long ladder was attached to the side of the tunnel. Johnny flicked on a switch on the inside of the tunnel wall and lights led all the way down and through a straight pathway.

"This will lead us to the hotel. There are many different passageways that lead to different areas of the Excelsior. When the time comes, we will break up and meet at the Presidential Suite. Now whatever you do, try to avoid any confrontations with the guests. I want all casualties to be against Dominick's men. Is everyone agreed?" Johnny asked.

"Yes, Boss," everyone shouted out.

Johnny and Frankie climbed down the ladder first. All the men followed except for a few guarding the cars and gate. A green light shone off the walls of the long tunnel. The tunnel allowed all the men, including six-foot-seven Two Toes, to run comfortably without banging their heads on the top. The tunnel moved slightly up until they reached an underground room. One set of elevators stood at the back wall of the metal room.

"This must have cost you a fortune," Frankie said with a laugh.

Johnny snorted. "My dad built it before he died. He said it was for presidents, royalty and anyone who mattered. Ultimately, it was a great way for him to escape in case anything went wrong. No blueprints were ever made for this entrance, and the men who made it live in Tahiti."

"Smart man," Frankie said.

Johnny pushed the button and the elevator doors opened. It could only fit six men at a time.

"Butch, Mickey, Snake Eyes, Knuckles, Jimmy, and Little Mo, hit seventh floor. That will take you to the kitchen. Pete, Bobby, Flat Head, Slugger, Buddy, and Louie twelfth Floor. The passage will take you to the Ballroom. Make sure no one sees you. I need Fat Head, Lucky, Rat, and Singer to get to the roof. The rest of you spread out in threes on each floor. Except for Frankie, Two Toes, Fist, and myself. We are heading to the Presidential Suite. Take out who you can and meet on the roof," Johnny commanded the group to their stations.

"Sure thing, Boss," they said together.

Johnny's group went through the elevator last. Everyone was silent in thought. All Johnny could think about was getting Isabella out alive and well. He had made her a promise, and Johnny always kept his promises. Everyone knew that. He wanted to kill Dominick more than he had wanted to kill Finn. The elevator doors buzzed and opened, allowing everyone to pack in. The boys were definitely of sound size and they looked like a pack of sardines in a metal can.

"Frankie, if I don't make it out tonight, it's all yours," Johnny said.

"Boss, you ain't gonna die tonight," Fist said with determination.

Frankie kept his eyes on the doors. He didn't say anything. All he did was nod his head. Things were quiet the rest of the way up. The boys had a variety of weapons in their hands. Fist was in front, gun ready for anyone who came in sight. The elevator buzzed again before the doors opened. They were in a dark space. Johnny flipped the switch on the right wall. Dim lights turned on and showed a long, narrow hallway. At the end you could see a wooden door.

"Boys, this is where we line up. Can't fit more than one at a time," Johnny whispered.

Johnny led the way. No one made a sound. Muffled noises could be heard. The closer they came to the door, the better they could hear voices. Suddenly, a loud thump and a high-pitched cry came through the door. The sound of her cry rang in Johnny's head. Johnny cracked the door open gently. The door was hidden behind a large mirror that led into the walk-in closet. Johnny slowly stepped in and motioned for the boys to stop and wait.

He could hear Dominick yelling in the background. "No matter how much you fight, you will always belong to me!"

"I do not belong to anyone, especially not to a psychopath like you!" Isabella yelled back.

Dominick grabbed her shoulders hard and shook her. Isabella punched him as hard as she could in the gut. Dominick only laughed. He pulled her into him and kissed her.

"Get off of her now, Dominick!" Johnny said as he stepped into the room, his M60 held in front of him.

Isabella caught him off guard and bit a hole straight through his lip. It matched the bandaged cut above his right eye. She followed the attack with a stomp from her high heel that gouged his foot. He screamed in pain as blood ran down his chin. He landed a strong punch to Isabella's face. She dodged and the punch knocked her shoulder out of place. She screamed in pain but brought up her knee to his groin. She ran into Johnny's arms. He held her with an iron grip and kissed her head. Dominick heaved on the floor as he held on to his manhood. Johnny pulled Isabella behind him and stuck the gun into the back of his head.

"Sweet dreams, Mr. Crillo," Johnny snarled.

"You might want to rethink your move, Boss," Lucky said behind them.

Johnny turned and saw Lucky holding Vinnie Carmine, with a knife to his throat. Vinnie was not able to stand on his own from the beaten he suffered. His chest heaved for air. Isabella stifled a cry. Others from Dominick's gang piled into the room.

"Daddy?" Isabella asked, her voice trembling with rage and terror.

"Fine, baby girl," Vinnie wheezed and coughed blood onto the floor.

"You lying sack of shit," Johnny said to Lucky.

"Oh don't feel too bad, Boss. You had to know this day was coming. You think I was going to put my life on the line for the rest of my life? Just remain as poison control? Hell no. Dominick is giving me more than you ever did," Lucky said.

He pressed the knife into Vinnie's throat until droplets of blood dripped down his neck.

"Put the gun down," Lucky said to Johnny. The other boys picked Dominick off the floor.

"I will rip you in half, asshole, if you move that blade another hair!" Isabella growled.

Lucky laughed. Dominick stood up on his own again and stood in front of Johnny.

"So you have your women do the fighting, huh, Johnny Boy? You're just like your father, weak," Dominick sneered.

Isabella started after him, but Johnny held her back. He stared at Dominick.

"My father was many things, but weak was not one of them. If anyone's father was weak, it was yours. He took you and your mother from your homeland. He let your mother die for the sake of a twenty-dollar bet," Johnny said.

Dominick ground his teeth in a fake smile.

"At least I didn't kill perhaps the one man who loved me more than your father ever did," Dominick said.

"What?" Johnny asked.

"Oh, so you didn't know. To make the story short and sweet, your father was dying from cancer. He hid it well, Finn made sure of it. Your father was too weak to fight, so he asked Finn to end his life. They fought over it for weeks, until finally Finn agreed. He killed your weak, pathetic father, and all for you. You inherited everything because of Finn. He wrote the deed and helped your father make the kingdom you have, until today. And the best part, you killed him. You killed the only man who ever truly cared for you. Wonderful, isn't it?" Dominick said with glee.

The other men chuckled with him.

Johnny looked out the window. The only thing that came to his mind was what Finn had taught him. *Don't let anyone ever get into your head, Johnny Boy. That's instant death. There are sad things you will face in this world.*

84

The thing you have to remember, kid, get over it. Move on. Grieving gets you nowhere but a one-way ticket to your grave. Life will never be easy, but that's what makes it so damn fun.

Johnny took a deep breath. "Why don't we make things interesting then? Both of our fathers failed. The only way to redeem at least one of them is to fight. My deal to you, let's fight the good old way. No weapons. Just you and me until someone dies," Johnny challenged.

Dominick laughed. "This is too easy. What are the stakes?" Dominick asked.

"If I win, Isabella and her father are set free. Excelsior is mine, and you're dead," Johnny said coolly.

"And when I win?" Dominick asked.

"Everything that belongs to me, is yours," Johnny said.

"Agreed," Dominick said.

Just as soon as he said it, Dominick lunged for Johnny. He picked him off the floor and slammed him into the wall. Johnny let out a loud grunt. The crash had broken a few ribs. Johnny slammed his fists into the side of Dominick's head. Dominick lost concentration, which allowed Johnny to maneuver his left arm around Dominick's neck. Dominick's face grew beet red from asphyxiation. Dominick flung his body around wildly, but Johnny's grip was iron. Johnny was able to get him pinned on the floor. Dominick reached for Johnny's eyes but missed, so he slammed his head up against Johnny's chin. Johnny's chin split open and his blood seeped onto Dominick's head. Just as Dominick's face turned purple, Lucky dropped Vinnie and came after Johnny with the knife. Isabella picked up Johnny's M60 and let a round of bullets go into Lucky's chest. Johnny's men swarmed into the room and began rampaging through Dominick's men. Isabella ran to her father and held his head in her lap.

Johnny held Dominick in his headlock until his pulse went silent. It wasn't until Frankie placed his hand on Johnny's shoulder that he realized Dominick "The Hammer" Crillo was dead.

***

One year later, Johnny and Isabella sat together on a beautiful tropic beach. The waves rolled up onto the shore. He held her hand and looked out at the water. The wind blew her hair around her shoulders. She turned to look at him. She stroked his face with her left hand. Her wedding ring sparkled in the sunlight. He smiled.

"Yes, my *cara mia*," Johnny whispered in her ear.

She pulled him toward her and kissed him. Nothing in the world had felt so right to him. She rolled on top of him and laughed. He rolled her onto her back in the sand and kissed her passionately again.

"Get a room!" Finn said.

Johnny looked up at Finn's scarred face. He had a fruity drink in his hand. He smiled as he took a sip.

"You know, we didn't give you guys your own half of the island for nothing," Johnny said.

"It makes me want to vomit every time I see it," another familiar voice said.

"Daddy, we can ship you two back if you'd like a change of scenery!" Isabella teased.

Johnny sat up and pulled Isabella with him.

"Why don't you both go to Tiki Island for a while? I hear there are plenty of willing girls there. Even for a couple of geezers like you two," Johnny said with a laugh.

"Why would I bring the buzzkill over here? The last girls we had flown over swam in shark-infested waters all the way back to America because of his love techniques," Finn said, pointing to Vinnie.

"You're like a whiskey hoedown, my friend, where as I am a champion of the tango, or king of the salsa!" Vinnie said as he danced in his flip-flops.

A helicopter pulled onto the far side of the island. Vinnie and Finn looked up with excitement. Isabella rolled her eyes in disgust.

"You both are pigs! To think of what Mama ever saw in you is beyond me," Isabella said.

"Actually, this time they are more our age. Frankie said we would really like them," Vinnie said with slight offense.

"How did Frankie say things were going at the hotel, sweetheart?" Isabella asked.

"Just peachy, my little flower petal," Finn mocked. The boys laughed. She threw her sandal at him.

"Finn, you know how our agreement was you give me something, I give you something right?" Johnny asked Finn.

Finn looked at him quizzically.

"I'm sure you'll recognize her when she steps out, but just in case you've gone senile, I thought you should know Anna is visiting," Johnny said with a smirk.

Finn's mouth dropped open. Johnny and Vinnie laughed. Vinnie took his finger and shut Finn's mouth for him.

"Don't worry, I'll take good care of Casanova here," Vinnie replied. He wrapped his arm around Finn and the two of them walked off to the helicopter.

"What are we going to do with those two?" Isabella sighed. "Who's Anna?" she asked.

"She is his true love. They almost eloped, but her father found out and took her to another country. One of those stories. He hasn't seen her in forty years or more," Johnny replied, smiling.

"How did you find her?" Isabella asked.

"I have my ways. Oh, by the way, Frankie said the new hotel is going up with ease and everything else is copacetic. He finally found someone too," Johnny said.

"Oh, thank God!" Isabella laughed.

Johnny laughed with her. He pulled her close to him again and kissed her lips gently.

Johnny looked into her eyes. "I do every day."

5

A SECOND CHANCE IN VEGAS

Tina DeSalvo

Chapter One

The 1960s Las Vegas Strip landmark Excelsior Hotel and Casino was pure luxury and warmth with the over-the-top shimmer that was expected from this town. Rachel Bienvenu stood in its elegant, cream-colored marble and dark walnut lobby, forcing her attention to shift from the grandeur to three of her four travel companions. Her mother, Ruby, the fourth of their group, was at the check-in desk, leaving her to keep an eye on the others, and rightly so. They were prone to wander, get lost, and get into trouble.

These three feisty women hadn't noticed the exquisite flower arrangements in four-foot marble vases surrounding them. They hadn't noticed the glistening gold-and-silver-tiled dome above them inscribed with a mosaic banner that read "Excelsior!" with three words beneath it: *Onward. Upward. Higher.* They hadn't noticed those beautiful things and the rest of the amazing décor around them because they were focused on plotting their activities for the next four days.

As their chaperone, Rachel wasn't too concerned with their plans; they had limitations and they'd be easy to spot. They intended to wear a different matching pink top each day—today was a solid bubblegum pink shell and cardigan—and they intended to wear their homemade, bedazzled white sashes, now hanging askew across their chests. The shiny silver, plastic, and rhinestone tiaras on their freshly styled heads would also make them easy to spot.

Yes, Rachel understood that they'd stand out against the sophisticated color palette of the Excelsior. She'd bet that there wasn't another group of sparkling sash- and tiara-wearing blue-haired, eighty-plus-year-old ladies in matching pink blouses there.

"What happens at a Vegas bachelorette party, stayz in Vegas," Tante Izzy, the ringleader of the group, cheered. Her excitement didn't make her Cajun accent heavier; it was always that way. "Dis is goin' to be da best bachelorette party ever!" They started to high-five each other, their old bones not allowing their hands to reach quite as high as they once had. "Thank you, Thelma, for getting married... again."

Rachel pulled her phone from the back pocket of her skinny jeans and took a few candid photos of the ladies. She was glad she'd decided to wear her comfortable, turquoise, peasant blouse that was both stylish with the bold, exposed zippers over the slanted chest pockets, and easy to move in because of the free-flowing fabric. She'd been doing a lot of moving, helping with luggage and herding the wandering ladies. Her choice of her comfy d'Orsay pointed-toe, cognac leather flats proved to be right too. Her feet didn't ache keeping up with these ladies who had an abundance of energy, spirit, and joie de vivre.

She was concerned about their fearlessness though. As a 911 operator in their small hometown of Cane, Louisiana, she'd witnessed the failed results of their fearless attempts more than once. It was why she'd volunteered to come to Las Vegas on eighty-two-year-old Thelma Breaux's bachelorette party. The bridesmaids, Louise Guidry and Rachel's aunt, Tante Izzy Bienvenu, had overambitious ideas of how to celebrate the end to Thelma's single life.

"Watch out, Vegas, here we come. Ayeee," Tante Izzy shouted and a hush fell over the noisy lobby full of once noisy guests. A few even froze mid-stride until they realized the old lady was celebrating and not having a seizure.

"Her declaration was more wishful thinking than warning," Rachel told her mother, Ruby, who stood next to her reapplying the reddish-orange lipstick that exactly matched her hair and jean jacket.

"I wouldn't be so sure," she said on a sigh. "Look at them, checking out that Excelsior employee walking past them. Dear Lord, did Thelma just whistle at him? I had no idea she could do that with dentures."

Rachel laughed. "Harmless fun."

"They may look harmless standing there all cute in their orthopedic shoes, but it's a farce." She shook her head. "Harmless fun. I'll throw those words back in your face when we are bailing them out of the Las Vegas jail. With women named Thelma and Louise hanging out with your crazy aunt, we are destined for trouble." Ruby groaned and tapped her way over the slick marble floor on three-inch narrow heels. She was in a hurry to get to the threesome who were blowing kisses to the concierge standing behind his walnut and gold inlay desk. *"Ne pas le faire."* Telling them *don't do that* in their first language, Cajun French, was no more impactful than saying it in Zulu.

"Don't you mess dis up fer us," Thelma said. "I'm about to get a date wit dat man over dere."

"Oh, no you won't," Ruby scolded. "He's young enough to be your grandson."

"And I'm old enough to be his mistress."

"Lordy," Ruby sighed. "We have to wait another hour for our suite. Let's go to the coffee shop and regroup."

"An hour?" Tante Izzy opened her black, red, and white sequin tote bag decorated with an appliqué of all four queens from a deck of cards. She handed Ruby two nickels. "Go play da slots. Meet us back here then."

Ruby looked at the two nickels in her palm, then turned to Rachel and waved her in closer. "Even if this could occupy my time for an hour," she told Tante Izzy. "I'm not letting you three flirts out of my sight."

"Youz momma is all huffy because of da man-on-pause," Tante Izzy told her niece. "When youz get dat, youz get all sweaty and moody. And worst, youz take a pause on da man."

"She needs a prescription for hair-moans," Thelma said to Louise, who was standing next to her. Louise smiled, but didn't answer. Thelma let go of her cobalt blue walker and grabbed her friend's ear. "I knew it. Youz ain't wearin' youz hearin' aid."

Louise swatted her hand away. "I bathe every day. And I use baby powder too."

"Aid. Aid," Thelma shouted. "Not bathe." She turned to Tante Izzy. "I refuse to share a room with someone who cain't hear. I'm roomin' with you."

"But youz snore. Dat's why youz are roomin' with Louise. She won't hear it."

"You gotz dat right," Louise said, although she clearly didn't know what everyone was talking about. Then she pointed to a man who was walking by, wearing faded jeans and a form-fitting black T-shirt. Tante Izzy and Thelma started blowing kisses to him, but he didn't notice. He stopped at the closest blackjack table and took a seat. "Nice derrière." Louise's voice seemed to echo off the marble floors and bounce off the heavily veined marble columns. Everyone, but the man her comment was intended for, looked at her.

"I think he's hard of hearing too," Rachel said, and laughed.

"Or wisely ignoring the catcalls coming from a blue-haired lady with a cane," Ruby added.

"Norman Landry?" Tante Izzy said, more to herself than anyone else.

Thelma's head jerked to the man at the blackjack table. "It does look like Norman," she agreed, pulling off her wire-framed glasses. "He hasn't left Cane since his daughter-in-law died from da breast cancer."

"Yes, he has. I heard he visited his grandson in prison," Ruby said.

"Norman must've dyed his hair dat pretty dark color," Thelma said. "Not dat I minded his white hair. He's handsome."

"Shame on you," Tante Izzy scolded. "Youz is engaged to Pete. He's got white hairs too. Not more than a dozen, but dey'z white."

Rachel looked at the man they were talking about. She knew Norman Landry. She knew Norman Landry's son, Raymond too. But she knew Raymond's son, Dante, best. Her heart started to thud. Man, she hadn't seen Dante since he left Cane the day after high school graduation. She'd heard he ended up in prison for robbing some big corporation about five years later. She didn't know the details of the theft nor did she know if he was still in prison.

She preferred to think of him as the badass rebel without a cause who drove fast cars with his music too loud and who'd stolen her heart when she was a sophomore. He'd stolen it without a kiss or a kind word, although she did get an unforgettable kiss later. He'd stolen it with a single act he didn't even know she'd witnessed. She'd been walking from the Sugar Mill Plantation onto the country road, when she spotted his shiny black muscle car. Suddenly, he slammed on his brakes, got out of the car in the middle of the two-lane highway, and picked up a skinny, matted, stray dog where it was cowering near a roadside ditch. Then he surprised her when he placed the ugly, dirty animal, with tenderness and care, into his precious car. She'd later seen him with the little mouse-colored mutt. Everyone did. The dog went everywhere with him from that day forward.

She stared at the man the ladies thought was Norman. He tapped the table and the dealer dealt him a card, then another. This man seemed taller, broader, more muscular than the boy she remembered—the boy who had kissed her senseless in the sugarcane fields near Sugar Mill Plantation just two days before he left town.

But dear Lord, it was him... maybe. Her body sure seemed to think it was. No one had ever made her pulse race or her flesh heat like Dante Landry. Maybe it was just her body reacting to the possibility that it was the guy she'd thought she was in love with fifteen years ago.

Regardless who this man was, she appreciated his flexing biceps as he picked up his cards. This man obviously worked out. A lot. That was something she admired, being a gym junkie herself. The Vacherie Sheriff's Office had an excellent gym for its employees. As a 911 operator, she had access to the facility. Had he gotten that body from the prison gym?

Really, Rachel. This man can't possibly be Dante.

"You ladies are delusional," Ruby said, trying to return logic to the group. "Norman didn't dye his hair black. That's ridiculous. He must be wearing a wig."

"A wig?" Rachel laughed. Her mother was buying into the fantasy that this man was the long-retired sheriff's deputy of Vacherie parish.

"I'm hungry," Louise said, not following the conversation she couldn't hear. "Let's eat Mexican."

"I don't like Mexican food," Thelma said, frowning. "I want soup. I've got to keep my girly figure for da weddin' night."

"Your girly figure iz long gone, Thelma," Tante Izzy said, pointing toward her friend's feet. "So are youz ankles."

"Tante Izzy!" Ruby, always the mediator, shook her head. "Be nice."

Rachel looked toward the blackjack table again. Yeah, there was something familiar about him, but...

"Oh my God." Did she just see the man that might be Dante Landry scratch his ankle and pull a card from under his pant leg? "Oh my God. He just cheated."

Ruby grabbed her arm. "Norman?"

"Yes, Norman." Rachel took her phone from her back pocket and started to video him. "Look. Look. He's doing it again."

Rachel continued to video, not noticing that Tante Izzy and Thelma had headed to the table, until she saw them in her viewfinder. Thelma bashed into the man with her cobalt walker. Tante Izzy started to shout. "Citizen's arrest. Citizen's arrest."

Rachel handed her phone to her mother, who had just told Louise to remain standing next to her. "Keep videoing."

She ran to the table. They were poking a man who could possibly be an ex-con. He could hurt them. Tante Izzy grabbed the man's arm, reached into her sequin bag and pulled out a can of Mace. *Dear Lord, this is going to turn bad.* Rachel reached them, pulled her aunt's arm from the man. He jerked, trying to get out of the way, and somehow, between her shoving and throwing herself between him and Tante Izzy, he fell backward in his chair. Acting like she knew what she was doing, she jumped on top of him, grateful for the little bit of spandex in her tight jeans. He grunted, the small chair still under him. Now she had him pinned. She didn't want this muscular, hulk of a man getting up and going after the ladies. Hard muscle and fury lay beneath her. "Call security," she shouted to the dealer who was staring at them.

The man grabbed her waist with strong hands and started to lift her up as easily as if she were an infant. She punched him as hard as she could on the shoulder.

"Crap. That hurt, lady."

He didn't really sound wounded at all. It ticked her off, so she punched him again. He grabbed a handful of the long dark hair that had fallen in a curtain over her face as she started to swing blindly. *God, is he seriously going to pull my hair?* It felt too careful an action for that.

"Holy crap. Rachel Bienvenu." He let go of her hair.

She stopped mid-swing and sat hard on his stomach. He grunted again. She stared into the handsome, chiseled face that held hints of the teenage boy who'd rescued a vulnerable dog from the side of the road, and who'd given her her very first kiss in the cane field. "Dante." She smiled, looking down at him. "Dante."

Tante Izzy harrumphed from behind Rachel. "That's one way to make a citizen's arrest. I prefer usin' da Mace to sittin' on him and smilin'."

Tante Izzy's words brought her back to her senses. "What the hell were you doing? Cheating? Don't deny it, I saw the whole thing. That's got to be against the law in Las Vegas." She climbed off of him and looked at the people gathered around them. A security guard rushed forward, pulled Dante up off the floor. Dear Lord, he'd grown taller since high school. He had to be six-three now, she realized as the security guard, a half foot shorter, handcuffed Dante's hands behind him. As his arm was being pulled behind him, the cuff of his jacket rose above his wrist and Rachel got a glimpse of pink and black. What was it? A tattoo? She had no time to process it. From behind her someone snapped cold, hard metal on her wrists. A second later, she heard someone ask Tante Izzy and Thelma to come with them.

"You see, I told you. I told you," Ruby shouted, rushing over to them and pushing through the crowd. "I told you I'd have to bail Tante Izzy out of jail. I just didn't expect I'd have to bail my daughter too." She looked at Dante, who was staring at her now, smiling, his silver-blue eyes bright. "And you, young man, I'm not bailing out. I don't care if you aren't Norman Landry, and are his grandson."

Chapter Two

Excelsior's black-uniformed security officers brought the four of them into the casino's version of a holding cell, in a behind-the-scenes location away from the guests. Dante was familiar with it. More than familiar with it. He'd spent countless hours in places like this, including this one. He looked at his "cellmates" and felt a tightening in his chest. These people were from his hometown. From Cane. From the place that held painful memories. From the place that strangled him like a frayed, taut rope caught on debris in the bottom of the bayou. The people of Cane felt that way to him.

Everyone but Rachel.

Rachel Bienvenu. The sweet but tough kid who'd always had an uninhibited, untethered, nonjudgmental air about her. Her green eyes, Bienvenu green eyes, were never filled with expectations or criticisms. Just questions that she never asked. She was gazing at him now with that same expression. Dear Lord, he'd kissed her in the middle of the damn never-ending sugar cane fields when she'd looked at him that way before. He was supposed to be pulling her truck out of the mud where she'd gotten stuck. He'd recognized the curiosity in her eyes then too. Only she'd been curious about *him*. Not why in the hell he was cheating at the blackjack table.

"Does Norman knowz what you do for a livin'?" Tante Izzy asked. She looked the same as she did fifteen years ago, only smaller, frailer.

She was also just as nosy.

"*Grand-père* and my dad just visited me here last month."

"That wasn't her question," Rachel said, her eyes studying his.

"Pete cain't know I'm in da pokey," Thelma said, sounding distressed. Like Tante Izzy, she hadn't changed much over the years. "He'z my fiancé. I'm gettin' married."

Dante nodded. "So I read."

"Youz read my weddin' announcement in da local paper?" she asked with a funny smile that made her look like a little girl with wrinkles and blue hair. "It'z my favorite picture of Pete."

"Not the newspaper." He nodded toward her sash. "It says you're the bride."

"And I'm da bridesmaid," Tante Izzy said, lifting her sash. "Dey cain't arrest da bridesmaid."

"Ah, but they do it all the time here in Vegas."

"Harrumph." Tante Izzy frowned at him. "Well, Ruby's goin' to bail us out."

"Yes, Momma will, even though she pretends she won't. But she won't have to. When the security officers return, we'll tell them what happened and they'll let us all go." Rachel looked at Dante and shrugged. "Except you, of course."

Damn, she was still cute, and tough. Not exactly like when she was a kid. Yeah, that sweetness still was there, in her smooth, fair complexion and soft, light eyes. There was something more there too. It looked like life had been damn good to her.

He let his eyes slide over her but not linger. Yeah, she'd come into womanhood just fine. More than fine.

"Dante, whatever happened to your dog?" Rachel asked. He could see in her eyes that she really wanted to know. It pleased him that she remembered him.

"Mutt had a long and happy life." He nodded. "He was a good dog."

She smiled and her whole face seemed to glow with it. "Mutt. I never knew his name, but I thought of that sweet dog from time to time."

Did she think of me too?

The door opened and Tim Owen, the head of security, walked in. He looked at Dante, the two old ladies, and Rachel, and started to laugh.

Rachel stood and Dante caught the scent of her perfume; sweet, but not too sweet. Some sort of flower.

"Laughing seems very unprofessional." She reached into her blazer pocket and Tim jumped back. "I don't have a gun." She shook her head. She handed him a badge and Dante nearly fell on the floor.

"You're a cop?" He'd never have guessed she was in law enforcement, given the unjaded look in her eyes.

She shrugged, then looked at Tim. "I'm an employee of the Vacherie Sheriff's Office. I've taken an oath to uphold the law. And, as such, I have to tell you that this man is a cheat."

"Girlfriend of yours, Dante?"

"Ha, ha, ha. Funny."

"Oh, not that kind of cheater," Rachel said, eyes wide. "He was switching cards at the blackjack table."

"Yes, I know." Tim leaned against the white-painted cinder block wall.

"I wantz to makes my one phone call," Tante Izzy said, walking toward the head of security. "I wantz to call my lawyer. My nephew, Beau Bienvenu. He's in Louisiana, but he'll get me out da pokey."

"Me too," Thelma added. Then she pointed an arthritic finger to her sash. "I gotz to get out da pokey, Officer. I'm gettin' married."

"To Pete," Dante said, humor in his tone.

Tim smiled and looked at Dante. "Bachelorette party?"

"Yeah. Bachelorette party."

"What's going on here?" Rachel asked, her eyes darting between Dante and Tim. "Have we been punked?"

Tim shook his head. "No. Dante has. You want to tell them?"

Dante shook his head. "Nope."

"Tell us what?" Rachel asked, moving to stand in front of Dante. "You obviously aren't in trouble with the law, and neither are we."

"We'ze not?" Thelma clapped her hands, stood, and got her walker that was near the door. "Let's go Izzy. Our room has got to be ready now. I need a nap. Gettin' arrested is exhausting."

Tante Izzy moved to the door, but turned to speak to Tim. "I usually take my nap right after *Da Price Is Right*. Do youz know what time *Da Price Is Right* is on here, and what channel?"

"'Fraid not."

She nodded. "Let's go Rachel. We'ze been sprung."

Rachel looked at Dante, cocked her head and bit her lower lip. His heart began to pound hard in his chest. Damn, if she just looked at him and his body reacted this way, what in the hell would happen if he kissed that pretty lip she was biting? Not something he should find out.

"I don't know what's going on here, but I think we're owed an explanation."

When neither Tim nor Dante answered, she sat back on the hard white plastic chair.

"Youz coming or not?" Tante Izzy asked.

"Not."

"I'll escort you two ladies back to the rest of your friends." Tim walked to the door, and held it open.

"I'll meet y'all in the suite, shortly," Rachel told the ladies.

They nodded and walked away.

Dante moved his chair directly in front of Rachel. If they were going to have a conversation, he wanted to look fully in her eyes. To her credit she didn't flinch, move, or act like she was frightened, though something in her eyes said that she was.

"I'm not a cheater." He leaned forward, resting his elbows on his knees. It moved him closer to Rachel, to her scent. Big mistake.

"So what do you call sneaking a card from your pant leg and playing it?"

"Work."

"Driving a limo is work. Building a house is work. What *you* did is not work. It's a crime."

He laughed, "Darlin', what I do is most definitely work. Tim hired me to do it."

"Stop talking in cryptic sentences and just explain what happened."

"Let me look at your badge."

She reached into her pocket and handed it to him. It was heavy, clean, and shiny. It looked like it had never been banged up in an apprehension on a shell road or dented from a perp swinging a lamp or bat at it.

He looked at her and handed it back to her. "How long you've been with the sheriff's office?"

"Five years."

"Before that?"

"What does this have to do with what happened in the casino?"

He smiled. "Nothing."

"Before that I taught seventh-graders. Before that I went to college in North Louisiana." She folded one long, nicely-shaped leg under her. "And you? Before you became a cheater-for-hire, what did you do?"

"Security."

"Convenient for your criminal activities, I suppose."

He laughed. "Rachel, I'm still in the security business. I'm a consultant and security operations specialist. I go into casinos, retailers, wherever, and check how their security team is working and determine if their security equipment is up to par. If not, I get it working right."

Her smile was slow to bloom. "So you *were* working when you cheated at blackjack."

He smiled back at her. He couldn't help it. "Apparently badly, since you caught me on my first card." He shook his head. "Although the blackjack dealer and the team on security cameras missed it. That's something I'll have to evaluate."

She retrieved her phone from her blazer pocket, tapped on the screen and handed it to him. A video of him sitting at the table was playing.

He watched as he drew the second card from his pant leg and slipped it on the table, then withdrew a card that was there. He was purposely clumsy the second time to see if anyone would pick it up. One person had. Thelma rushed into view, ramming him with her walker, followed by Tante Izzy threatening a citizen's arrest and pulling out a can of Mace.

"Ah, here comes the cavalry," he said, as Rachel moved in and knocked him to the floor. The look on his face was surprise, turning to anger and then pleasure as he gathered her long, silken hair in his hand.

"I did go through police academy," she said. He handed her phone back to her and saw by a quick flicker in her eyes that she was either lying or had more to say. Since she had the badge with her name on it, he figured it was the latter.

"Would you mind sending me that video?" He gave her his phone number. She sent it to him. "Thanks. I need to ask you to do one more thing."

She leaned in toward him as he leaned on his knees. It hadn't been intentional, but now that she was so close, he realized he liked feeling her warm breath on his cheek. He looked at her smooth, full, bottom lip, barren of cosmetics, but a pretty pink nonetheless. She bit it, again. Dear Lord. He remembered her doing that in the cane fields so many years ago. He'd found it irresistible then and he did now. Crap.

"What do you want, Dante?" Her breath quickened. Her pupils dilated. She was as aroused as he was. The realization hit like being dropped in a cold bayou.

He stood, began to pace. "I want you to pretend you don't know me or see me if I run another op in the casino."

She stood, tucked her phone her back pocket. "I don't know you, Dante. Not really."

But he knew exactly who she was, he realized. He'd always known who Rachel Bienvenu was and how she made him feel.

He watched Rachel walk out the door behind him. She hadn't bothered saying good-bye.

Chapter Three

The forty-five-minute walk she'd taken around the resort hadn't eased her emotions. Rachel was angry. She had no right to be, but she was. For a moment, she'd thought he was going to kiss her. She'd seen in his silvery blue eyes that he wanted to. She'd heard it in the way he drew a breath. She should be happy he hadn't, not upset. What business did she have wanting to kiss a convicted thief, even an employed one with an exciting job? Even one she'd been half in love with as a teenager.

Stupid. Stupid. Stupid.

Rachel unlocked the suite door with the key she'd gotten from the front desk. She was greeted by the too-loud sound of the television in the living room. It wasn't *The Price is Right,* but it was a game show, *Pokeno,* from downstairs in the casino. Louise was sitting on the huge, U-shaped, royal purple sectional sofa watching it. Rachel's bed linens— two pillows, sheets, and a blanket—were stacked on the far side of her. The others were sharing the two bedrooms.

"Hello, Louise." She spoke loudly enough to be heard over the television.

"Hi, *chere.*" She waved without looking at Rachel. "Everybody is nappin'. I couldn't fall asleep. Thelma snores too loud. Like the engine of a freight train."

Rachel smiled and spotted her luggage near the door. She was glad it was there. She didn't want to have to poke inside the two bedrooms to find it while the others slept. She walked into the small kitchenette and spotted a large fruit basket wrapped in cellophane; an attached card was still in the envelope. Rachel removed the cellophane, took a banana, and sat at the small maple dining table. As she chewed, she removed the card and read it.

"Sorry, Dante."

Her heart began to pound. She'd expected the basket to be from hotel hospitality, not the guy she'd sat on in the casino. The guy she had dreamed of in the very best dreams since she was a teenager. Who knew he was this thoughtful. She did.

She tossed the banana peel away and started to go into the living room, but the television was much too loud. She grabbed a pillow and walked out onto the large balcony adjacent to the living room. The desert heat smacked her in the face instantly. It stole her breath and made her flesh prickle. She closed the door behind her.

She slipped off her shoes and dropped onto the lounge chair in a sliver of shade, and propped the pillow behind her head. She looked out over the balcony to the expansive pools surrounded by multi-level stone terraces and cascading waterfalls. There must've been two hundred people in and out of the pool, enjoying, or tolerating, the brutal heat. She imagined how cool and refreshing the water must feel. Rachel scanned the people around the pool and her eyes landed on a man whose lips she'd wanted on hers less than an hour before.

Dante.

His shirt was off. She was too far for details, but she could see his well-formed body. Wide shoulders tapered to narrow hips. A pretty blonde in a white bikini sat in the lounger next to him. Was she his girlfriend? Wife?

She shook her head. None of her business. If she were in Cane, she wouldn't have a thought about him.

Except, that wasn't really true. Whenever she saw a stray dog, or heard music blaring from a muscle car, she remembered him. She remembered his restlessness and his tenderness.

He moved from the lounge chair into the pool. As he swam to the bar, the woman in the white bikini moved to sit next to another man. Good. Dante ordered a drink. When the bartender turned to make it, Dante reached over the bar and stole a handful of money from the large tip jar. He stuffed it in his bathing suit pockets. Rachel threw back her head and laughed. "He's working again." What a fun job.

Ruby opened the sliding door. "Oh, dear Lord. It feels like a hot flash out here." Her mother stepped outside. "What has your attention?" She leaned over the balcony.

"Dante," Rachel said, a smile on her lips. "He's working again."

Ruby shaded her eyes and spotted him. She looked a moment, then looked at Rachel. "Call security. Hurry. He's a petty thief."

Rachel laughed. "Not exactly." She decided not to tell her mother about his job. She wasn't sure Ruby could keep his secret.

***

They had tickets to a new variety show at the Excelsior that was a spin-off from a very popular television talent show. Thelma was especially excited about attending. She insisted they eat dinner early, despite the show being three hours later. So, at five, dressed in evening clothes, they walked into Louis's Steak House, named after the casino founder, Louis "The Lip" LaFica.

Tante Izzy, Thelma, and Louise all wore sequined floor-length gowns in various shades of pink. Although they were overdressed for the occasion, the homemade bride and bridesmaid sashes and plastic tiaras seemed to balance their outfits and made them look adorable, if not, costumey. Her mother just looked lovely wearing a hot-flash ready, light cotton maxi-dress with large, orange hibiscus flowers on it. Her shawl was the same color as the hibiscus. Her shoes, of course, were high, spiked, and ridiculously hard to walk in. And *orange*.

It was because of her mother's unnecessary suffering with impractical shoes that Rachel had developed a fondness for pretty flats. Tonight she wore silver leather flats that had a deep scoop over her toes, creating nice toe-cleavage. The scoop matched the front and back neckline of her pale silver chiffon cocktail dress that draped in a soft puddle down her torso to a few inches above her knees. The scoop gave her a modest cleavage at her breasts. She didn't have time to fix her hair in any special way, so she wore it straight down her back.

As they were escorted to their table, Rachel spotted Dante sitting alone in one of the four, large, five-star private-dining wine rooms she'd read about on the restaurant website. Each was named after winning hands of Louis LaFica's favorite game—poker. According to the plaque on the door, Dante was seated at a long, dark walnut, rough-hewn table in the *Royal Flush* room. Rachel thought he looked appropriately regal, handsome and a bit dangerous in his black double-breasted suit, with a black, silk, crewneck T-shirt. She caught his eye as she passed, remembering that he didn't want her to acknowledge him when he was working. Was he working now? He lifted a brow and gave her a half smile. They hadn't been sitting for more than five minutes when he walked up to their table.

"Ladies. You're still on Louisiana time? Having an early dinner."

"No, just senior-citizen time," Ruby said, looking uncertain whether to invite him to join them, or call security.

"We goin' to da early *Talent USA* show," Tante Izzy said.

"It has great reviews. I think y'all will like it." He placed a bottle of wine on the table. Then another. "A white and a red. Both excellent wines. I hope you enjoy them." He walked around the table to Rachel. He leaned in to talk to her. His fragrance—citrus, cedar, a hint of bay rose, and masculinity—wafted over to her. "I know you have dinner plans," he said, his voice just above a whisper. Her mother scooted forward from across the table, straining to hear. She looked worried. Rachel signaled her with a blink and nod that everything was fine. Ruby didn't relax. "Would you join me for a before dinner drink at my table? You can rejoin everyone before the entrées are served."

Rachel stood and Dante straightened. "Please excuse me," she said, speaking directly to her mother. "I'm joining Dante for a glass of wine. Momma, please order the sea bass for me."

"I don't think…"

"No, youz don't," Tante Izzy interrupted and waved at Rachel to go.

"Thank you for letting me borrow her, Ruby, Tante Izzy and…" He paused and smiled, his eyes twinkling. "Thelma and Louise. You two stay out of trouble, now."

The older ladies laughed aloud at his movie reference. They were totally charmed by him. Her mother was not.

As they walked away, they heard Thelma gushing. "Oh, young love," she said almost singing it. "I remember my first husband. We were young and in love."

"Youz got dat right," Louise said. "Youz were fifteen."

"I'm not sure about this," Ruby said, staring at Dante and Rachel's backs.

"She needz to spend time wit someone her own age. Even if he'z an ex-con."

"Ex?" Ruby's voice squeaked. "He'll be a con again when the police come to arrest him."

Rachel's heart was racing, her head felt light as Dante took her hand and led her into the private room. She was totally charmed by him too. He closed the door behind them. She spun around, looking at the back-lit bottles of wine shelved on every wall from floor to ceiling. "I feel drunk just looking at all of this."

"Me too."

Rachel turned to face him and found him staring at her. His eyes were heavy and intoxicating. Instead of leading her to sit at the table where two empty glasses were already set, he tugged on her hand until he brought her to the corner of the room, out of view of anyone looking through the glass door. He spun her around, his hand grasping hers between their chests. "Rachel, I know this seems out of left field, but since we were in the security office I've been thinking about us in the cane field when you ran your car off the road."

"I didn't run it off the road, I was avoiding hitting a nutria."

"I was glad I was the one who found you walking on the side of the road carrying two of your hubcaps." He smiled and Rachel was sixteen years old again. "Why was that?" She laughed, feeling young and silly. "I found them as I was walking out of the cane field. I didn't want to lose them. My dad would've been furious and made me go to Hubcap Annie's and use my money to buy new ones."

"Holy crap. I haven't thought of Hubcap Annie's since before I left Cane."

Rachel's stomach pinched. "Why did you leave Cane without telling anyone good-bye? Not me, of course, but the guys you hung around with? Your father?"

He let go of her hand and sat on one of the navy velvet dining chairs. "Exactly for this reason. People were always gossiping about me. Hell, look how you know that I left town without telling anyone other than my grandfather." He grabbed her hand again and pulled her closer to him. She looked down at him and saw the pain in his eyes.

"Was the gossip so awful for you?"

"How do you do that, Rachel?" He swallowed hard and she knew his emotions were high. "We didn't hang around in high school, but I noticed you. And, what I saw in your eyes and actions was something deeper than the other kids. You always had a depth of understanding… of others, of yourself. And unlike most everyone else in town, you saw *me*, not the son of the man who grieved for his wife so hard that he ignored his kid, or the poor boy who watched his mother lose her battle with breast cancer after getting it three damn times. I guess that's why I wanted to kiss you that night in the cane fields. I wanted to be kissed by someone who actually knew who she was kissing."

He stood and for reasons she couldn't explain, she thought of the colors she'd seen near his wrist. She took his right arm and turned it, then pushed up the sleeve of his black sports coat. He didn't resist.

"Oh, Dante." She exposed the tattoo, and in doing so, his heart.

Her throat clogged with emotions. "For your mother?"

He nodded and she gently ran her finger over the pink, breast cancer ribbon, outlined in black. Beneath it were the words *Always Fight for a Second Chance.*

"A reminder… " he began, but Rachel interrupted him.

"To not give up."

He shook his head. "No." He looked away, withdrawing.

"Please tell me what this tattoo is a reminder of." She touched his cheek and he turned to look into her eyes. She felt the sadness within him.

"This is a reminder to me of my mother's last words as I held her in my arms while she took her last breath." He gripped her hand tightly within his. "I want to always remember that moment. It was a gift she gave to me, Rachel. Just me. My dad couldn't have accepted the gift and seen how special it was." He swallowed hard. "She asked me to hold her and encircle her with love so she could pass feeling joyful and secure into God's embrace. Her last words were, '*always fight for a second chance.*'"

Tears welled in her eyes. "And have you?"

He took a step closer to her. "I think so." He was within a whisper of her mouth. She felt his breath on her mouth. "Maybe not always," he whispered.

His lips pressed softly onto hers, as gentle and tender as she remembered them to be when they were teenagers but with more finesse. His tongue explored and lured like nothing she'd experienced before, even with him. She lifted her hand to his cheek as the kiss deepened. His body pressed against hers until she felt every muscle, every pulse, and how much he desired her. His hand released hers and slid down her back, gentle at first and then with more urgency. He gripped her dress in his fist. His mouth trailed a wet, hot path down her neck. She lifted her chin giving him more access and sighed.

He grabbed her derrière and squeezed. "I thought a kiss would be enough. Like I had thought it would be enough in the cane filed." His voice was deep, raspy.

She shook her head, no.

"No, not enough or no, you don't like what I said?"

"Both."

He looked at her, his pupils dilated, leaving only a sliver of blue around them. He kissed her once more, this time with less heat. He stepped back and she started to reach for his lapel to pull him back to her, but then remembered where they were. Who they were.

"Would you like some wine?"

She nodded, unable to speak yet.

Even though there was an open bottle on the table, he stood on the chair and stretched until he pulled a bottle from its resting place. The label was faded, old.

"Are you working?" she asked.

His answer was a half-smile. Oh, he was working, playing a thief and enjoying himself.

He opened the wine and poured them each a glass. He placed the bottle on the floor where someone passing wouldn't see it. She glanced around the room for the security cameras that would've seen the theft and their kiss. There were none. He must've been checking on the competence of the wait-staff.

She sat. He handed her the glass of clear, deep purplish wine. "To our second chance kiss," he said. They clinked their glasses together.

"Tastes really good," she said, after taking a sip.

"I'd like to take credit, but it's purely random." They laughed. "So you didn't like teaching seventh-graders?"

"Speaking of random—so is that question." The door opened and Dante waved the waiter off. "No. I did not. I didn't have a calling for it. It takes a special person to teach."

"Is law enforcement a calling for you?"

She shrugged. She hated not telling him the truth of her work as a 911 operator. She wasn't embarrassed by it. She liked it very much. She just didn't feel she wanted to reveal everything about herself to him. She felt exposed already. Telling him about her day-to-day life while they were in this magical place was, well, too real. It was illogical, especially when they'd shared something very real when he exposed his raw emotions about his mother. That kiss felt real too. And enchanting.

"I often work on projects that I enjoy at Sugar Mill Plantation," she offered, finding a topic that felt safe. "You remember Sugar Mill, don't you?"

"How can I not? It's the largest, proudest, most historic plantation in Cane. Your family has been tied to it for generations."

"It roots us to Cane."

"I've seen it in some star-studded movies lately."

She laughed. "Yeah? That's the projects I'm talking about. My new cousin, Elli, she married Ben… " She looked at him to see if he remembered her cousin, Ben; when he nodded she continued. "Elli was an Academy Award–winning movie producer. She doesn't produce anymore, but she works with movie productions that want to film at Sugar Mill. I've worked as a local locations coordinator."

"So I'd see your name in the credits?"

She smiled at the thought of him thinking about her when she was gone. "Yes." She told him the titles of the movies she'd worked on.

"I'll definitely look for your name." His tone was flat. She knew he was thinking about her leaving in just a few days, like she was.

"I'm glad I ran into you in the casino," Rachel said.

"You mean tackled me."

"You fell. I just made sure you didn't get up."

"You definitely did that." Rachel could tell by his tone that he wasn't talking about the incident at the blackjack table.

"You know, I had a serious crush on you in high school." Rachel couldn't believe she just blurted that out.

His eyes widened. "I had no idea." He lifted her chin and brushed his thumb over her heated cheeks. "How serious?"

"As serious as a teenage girl gets."

He leaned closer. She could smell the wine on his breath. "And now?"

She closed her eyes, trying to center her body that felt off kilter. "Oh, I don't know." But she did know, and now that she looked at him, his eyes told her he did too.

He kissed her then, his lips just barely touching hers. The tease and promise of what those lips could do made her want to crawl onto his lap and melt into his heated flesh.

A knock on the door broke the spell.

"Your meal is getting cold," Ruby said, her voice sharp. She left the door open and walked away.

"I think that's what it would've felt like if we had gotten caught making out when we were in high school."

She touched her forehead to his. "Not quite. My father would've taken you to the shed and tried to scare you off by sharpening his cane knife with the old leather strap."

They laughed.

Chapter Four

Dante stayed away from Rachel the next day. He knew it was best for her and for him. Having a Vegas fling would be wrong. He respected and cared for her too much to do that. It was odd to admit that, he realized, since they hadn't seen each other in nearly fifteen years and before that, never dated or hung around in high school... other than sharing a really sweet kiss in the moonlit sugarcane fields. But there were strong feelings that Rachel ignited in him that might've had roots in what he'd observed in her as a teenager. Whatever it was, it scared the hell out of him. It was bigger than anything he'd felt before.

He buried himself in working on the report for the Excelsior at his office. His employees asked him what was wrong when they saw how oddly he was acting. He told them nothing was wrong, but they didn't believe him. Neither did he.

He finished the report on the incident at the blackjack table, but needed to add Rachel's video to it. He downloaded it to the computer, and because he was thorough, he needed to watch it to make sure it had downloaded properly. He pressed play. Rachel's voice came on, telling her mother to keep videoing as she rushed into the frame to help Tante Izzy and Thelma. She was protective of the people she loved. She'd removed Tante Izzy from what Rachel perceived as danger and took the potential source of danger down so he wouldn't hurt the old ladies.

His longtime employee, Samuel, walked into the office just as he grabbed Rachel's hair on the video and said her name. She sat up, smiled, and said his name. He'd be damned if he didn't like the memory of her smiling down at him.

"That woman has it bad for you. Damn, the way she said your name was like it mattered." He dropped a file on his desk. "That woman is in love with you. Who is she?"

Dante didn't answer. He grabbed his car keys and left the office.

***

Rachel had helped Ruby get the ladies settled in for a five-star spa day. She wasn't in the mood to pretend she was relaxed and content when she wasn't. No amount of scented oil or Zen music would make her feel that way. She was a fool for letting her teenage feelings surface with a man she hadn't seen in fifteen years and wouldn't see again after she left Vegas. Surface. Yeah, her feelings had been there just below *the surface* all along. If she was honest with herself, how she felt about Dante had even been the secret benchmark she'd used for every guy she dated. Now, that benchmark had been raised. Her feelings felt stronger today than they had before they were in the Excelsior security holding room.

She returned to the suite, grateful she had three hours to herself. Before she could lock the inside deadbolt, she felt the air get warmer, lighter. She didn't turn around. "Dante."

She heard him suck in a breath. "How did you know?"

"I felt you." She inhaled deeply, hoping to find the strength to not turn around and beg him to hold her. God, she missed not seeing him the day before. She turned to face him where he stood near the sofa. "What are you doing here?"

"I don't know." He moved closer to her. "I do know." He shook his head. "It's insane. Illogical. Although it doesn't feel that way." He looked away and then back at her. The struggle was palpable.

"Go away, Dante. You clearly don't want to be here. Or you want to be here for some reason that lacks conviction."

"I'm certain. As certain as the sun rises. I'm just nervous as hell."

"Let me ease your nerves. I don't want to have a Vegas fling." A tear slipped down her cheek and she saw his face crumble. Was it because she was crying or because she rejected them having a fling?

He rushed up to her. "Don't cry, cheré. I don't want a fling, either," he whispered, kissing her tears. "Don't be sad." His lips closed over hers and she tasted the saltiness of her tears. Her arms came around his neck bringing him in closer. He changed the angle of the kiss and a deep guttural sigh rumbled inside him. Heat seared just under her skin at the sound of it. She shivered. "Kissing you feels so good." His words touched her heart, filling it with desire, need.

He'd said no fling. What was this, then? Whatever it was felt right and impossible to stop. She didn't wait for him to deepen the kiss; she did it, needing to share her passion with him. In turn, he gave her his. His mouth and tongue moved over the column of her neck, dipped into the cleavage of her white, drawstring cotton blouse. With his teeth he loosened the string, and the blouse fell open to her navel. Dante lifted her in his arms and carried her to the velvet sofa.

He gently laid her onto what felt like a royal purple cloud with the same tenderness he showed to that sweet stray he rescued. She shifted so he could lay on the sofa with her. As he did, his hands opened the fabric at her breasts and he lightly touched her right nipple with the tip of his tongue, just a taste, just a man savoring. He groaned his pleasure and she arched, gripping his hips, pulling his center to hers. He sucked in a breath. His hands now on her thighs, he paused. He looked into her eyes. She smiled and he smiled back. Her heart swelled in her chest. She loved this man so much. This was most certainly not a teenage crush or a Vegas fling.

He lowered his mouth to hers again as his hands slipped inside the opening at the bottom of her shorts. There he teased with a light scrape of his fingers over her panty, hinting at what pleasure he intended for her.

Rachel sat up, reached for the bottom of his shirt. He helped her remove it, before removing hers. He rested his hand over her heart, then took her hand to rest over his. "Right here it feels best." His voice was so thick with emotion it felt like a physical touch.

She kissed his bare chest, his nipples, the ribbed muscles on his abdomen before they removed the remainder of each other's clothes, except for her thin red lace panty. He pressed her back onto the sofa, kneeling on the floor next to her to feathering kisses on her torso, over the strip of lace between her legs, her thighs and calves.

"Please, Dante. Please."

He looked at her and smiled in the way that said he was still that sensitive, bad-boy she fell in love with as a teenager. She arched as he removed her panty and kissed her inner thighs, then joined her on the sofa. His weight was solid and real as he slid into her with a heavy groan. "Yes. This is how it's supposed to be."

They moved together, heart to heart, until their hearts pounded so hard she knew they were beating as one. Their bodies did too as they raced to the special moment that now linked them together forever as their first kiss had.

Chapter Five

Rachel lay on top of Dante as his nails gently scraped over her back. He knew that what they had was exceptional. How did he tell the woman he'd admired as a teenager that he wanted to be with her forever as adults?

"Rachel, don't go back to Cane." Crap, that wasn't what he wanted to say. "What I mean is… I know it seems fast, I mean to say, I never believed in love at first sight, but… Not that this is exactly what we have. We've known each other a long time." She eased up onto her elbows. "Hell, I'm not explaining myself well." He exhaled. "I love you, Rachel. Like the grow-old-together kind of love."

She kissed him gently on the lips. "This isn't fast for me. I've always loved you, Dante." She smiled and his heart flipped in his chest. "I'm happy you want me to stay, but we need to work out the you-live-in-Vegas-and-I-live-in-Cane thing. I can move away from Cane but I need to be part of my family's lives. They're important to me. Can you accept that? They're the very people you wanted to move away from."

He nodded. "I'm past that. I'm secure in who I am and I've grown to understand the people I thought I was running from. It wasn't because of them. It was because of my insecurities." He shrugged. "That was then. Now, I think my business needs to expand into South Louisiana. My family is important to me too."

Rachel hugged him so tightly, and with such love, that he finally understood his mother's words of wanting to be embraced in love, joy, and security. "Dante, I adore you. I don't care if you're an ex-convict."

Ex-convict? "I've never served time in prison. Why do you think I did?"

"Because that's what your grandfather said."

"Impossible. Why would he lie?" Dante reached for his cell phone in his jeans pocket on the floor. "Let's call him. I can't have the woman I intend to marry think I'm an ex-con when I'm not."

"Marry? You want to marry me?"   Her heart skipped a beat.

"Didn't I ask?" He put the phone on speaker.

"No. But if you do ask, I'll say yes."

"I figure we're in Vegas and you've already had a bachelorette party."

She laughed. "But I don't have a tiara and bride sash."

"Hello," his grandfather answered, his voice gravelly.

"*Grand-père*. I'm with the woman I love and she says there are rumors going around Cane that claim I've served time in prison. Do you know anything about that?"

"I thought dat was over." He cleared his throat. "I tole Lou at da diner dat you bought a security company for such a good price, you stole it from the previous owner. Well, da old gossips in da diner got it wrong and started tellin' everyone you were a thief. Then, as gossip goes, it wound up that you'd gone to prison because you stole from your boss."

"For the record, it wasn't *that* cheap and the man I bought it from retained ten percent ownership. He's very happy, since the company is ten times more profitable than when he had it."

"Glad to know," his grandfather said. "Now tell me bout dis woman you love. You said she told you about the rumors in Cane? She's been to Cane?"

"She lives in Cane. She's a cop there." Rachel's eyes widened.

"Ah, we need to talk," she whispered. "Now."

"What's her name?"

"Rachel Bienvenu."

"The nine-one-one operator?"

Dante looked at her; she was biting her bottom lip. "Yep, that's her." He noticed she was blushing too. "Gotta go, *Grand-peré*. We'll talk later." He disconnected the phone. "Rachel…"

"In my defense, I never said I was a cop." She forced a smile. "Just that I work for the sheriff's office. Honestly, I was going to tell you but…" He flipped her over and was now in the dominant position.

"You have our lifetime to tell me all the details of yours. I know all I need to know. I love you."

"Dante, your mother was right. We should always fight for a second chance. This is ours."

6

NEARLY NAKED

Sabrina York

Finally. Her work was done. Victoria Carstairs sighed heavily as she pressed the button for her floor in the lush Excelsior Hotel, the site of the annual Vegas tech conference her boss insisted on attending. She grimaced and lifted her foot and massaged her arches as she waited for the car to usher her up to the top floor.

Though her room was up in the ether with the rich and famous, she was neither. And though the top floor was speckled with fancy suites, she had a regular boring old room, one designated for the servants of those titans, so they could be close. So their masters never had to wait for service.

Not that she was bitter.

She wasn't. Not really.

She loved her job working for Mr. Savage—pronounced in the French form if one wanted to avoid a lecture from the owner of the company. As Mr. Savage's executive assistant, she enjoyed many perks, including exceedingly interesting tasks, parties in the stratosphere (though she attended to oversee the events, not enjoy them) and frequent trips in his personal jet. The only downside was the fact that she had to spend a lot of time with *him*.

He was a harsh taskmaster, treated her like a medieval serf, and when he didn't need her, acted as though she did not exist.

Though she could hardly blame him for that. Early on—when she'd been working her way through the ranks—she'd realized that to advance with the company, she needed to play a very specific part. A woman completely dedicated to her job. So dedicated to that work that she could not be bothered to make herself more than a Dowd.

Hence the black horn-rimmed glasses, tight bun and sartorial camouflage. Not a whit of her true self was represented in her bland gray suits and unattractive shoes. She restricted her passion for beautiful things to her private life. Silk chemises, lacy underwear and sexy nightclothes—all kept tightly under wraps.

It made her soul wail a little bit each time she donned her mask, but it was better this way.

She'd seen what could happen to a woman Mr. Savage noticed.

The elevator dinged and the door opened to a long, thickly carpeted hall. Tori nodded to the concierge as she slipped off her shoes and padded barefoot to her room.

It had been a hell of a day. She'd started before six a.m. to set up the conference and had been going nonstop since. Her boss had left at the end of the event—beaming at his success—but Tori had stayed to clean everything up. Now she was exhausted.

Damn.

Resolutely, she willed herself to shake off her malaise. She was in freaking Vegas. Her work was done. It was time for her to enjoy herself, by God. She'd take a nice refreshing bath, dress up—as herself—and go out on the town. She deserved a wild night of fun.

She did.

Of course, when she got into her room and flopped on the bed, she dozed off. Not for long, but when she awoke she was annoyed with herself. This was her only night in Vegas. She should be drinking cocktails, flirting with hot guys and winning millions on the slots.

But all she wanted was to curl up and sleep.

Not that her boss worked her to the bone like his own personal nerdy Cinderella, but she could really use a pumpkin and a fairy godmother about now.

A pity there were no such things. No magical wands. No enchanted shoes. No singing forest creatures.

But she could make her own magic. She would have one thrilling night of excitement and adventure before she packed her bags and returned to her desultory existence.

Determinedly, she made her way to the bathroom and turned the taps.

Tonight was her night.

She would have a wonderful time... or die trying.

She nearly fell asleep in the bath, but when she got out, the cold touch of the air-conditioning snapped her awake. She let down her hair, reveling in the thick curls she'd liberated. She loved the way they cascaded over her shoulders and down her back, but mostly she loved the release of the pinch of the bun. Her life was a pinched existence of late. More and more so each day as her spirit rebelled against the part she played.

Ah, but when she let down her hair... It was as though she had declared her freedom from Mr. Savage. The thought made her smile.

Thusly encouraged, she put on her face. She loved watching the transformation as she added highlights to her lids, thickened her lashes and painted a rich red on her lips.

It was like coming alive again.

And the dress... The dress she'd bought just for tonight. Short and sexy with a flirty skirt, it highlighted the length of her legs, the nip of her waist and the swell of her bosom. It made her feel like a sexy woman.

Oh, she knew she was a sexy woman, but she was so used to playing down her true nature, it *felt* like an awakening.

She twirled before the mirror and flashed herself a wicked smile.

Yes.

She was ready for whatever fate had in store tonight.

And whatever it was, she would grab it with both hands.

She slipped on her favorite shoes, a pair of heels festooned with blinding rhinestones and, after one last makeup check—or two— she grabbed her clutch and headed for the door, her heart light, anticipation sizzling in her veins.

With a deep breath, she stepped out into the hall, determined to—

Her thoughts scuttled as her gaze locked on a man standing in the hall.

In his underwear.

It took her a moment to realize who it was, because she'd left her glasses off—on purpose—and, of course, because she'd never seen Mr. Savage in his underwear. The sight made her brain fizzle and pop.

She'd always thought he was an insanely handsome man, but she'd never realized how broad his shoulders were, never witnessed the bulge of his biceps, never dreamed his abs were so ripped. He leaned

115

against the wall, arms crossed and eyes closed, as though he often relaxed, mostly naked, in a hotel hallway.

And he was, *mostly* naked. Except for his skivvies—boxers, which she found somewhat fascinating—and socks.

His eyes opened and she was, as always, stunned by that deep and dreamy blue. His lips quirked.

"Well, hello," he said. There was a thread there in his tone, one she'd never heard before... at least not directed at her. Something pleasant.

And... predatory. In a *good* way.

She tucked her clutch under her arm, but just to have something to do. Not that he made her skin prickle as he stood there like that, looking far too delicious. "Um... hello."

He nodded to his door. "I'm locked out."

"I see that." She shifted from one foot to the other. "Have you told the concierge?"

He blew out a breath. "He's not there right now."

"Well, that's a pity." She flashed him a smile and turned on her heel. This was *her* time, after all. "Have a nice night."

"Wait!"

Tori stopped short. She'd never heard a thread of panic in Mr. Savage's voice. It was... titillating. She glanced at him over her shoulder. "Yes?"

"Aren't you going to help me?" Aww. He sounded like a little boy, all pouty like that. Too bad she wasn't on the clock.

"I can let the front desk know you are out here."

He put out a lip. "Can't you at least lend me something to wear while I wait?"

She surveyed his person. "You look fine." He did.

"I'm half-naked."

"A little more than half," she suggested.

He set his hands on his hips—which made her lungs lock because his pecs rippled—and affected a glower. "Surely you are not going to leave me here like this?"

"I am. And don't call me Shirley."

It was an old joke, but he laughed at it. Whether that was a reflection of his humor or his desperation, she wasn't sure. "You can lend me your robe at the very least," he said in a pleading tone.

"I doubt my robe would fit you," she said.

"Still..." He shot her a piteous look, one that was so out of character for him, it made her blink in surprise. "You must have something that would work."

She did. As his assistant, she had a key to his room, but she had no inclination of letting him off that easily. Seeing him ill at ease was too tempting an opportunity to pass up.

So she turned back to her room and unlocked the door, though beyond anything she wanted to be on that elevator now, heading out for a night of sin, not rifling around in her suitcase for something her annoying boss could wrap around his dangly bits. But again... she could not pass up this chance to torment him. At least a little. She would give him her robe, wish him well and leave him there in the hall.

In her robe.

She hadn't expected him to follow her inside, but he did. She whirled on him and gasped. He filled the room with his presence. And he stole all the oxygen, the bastard.

She grabbed her robe and she tossed it to him.

He caught it and stared at it as though she'd just given him an aardvark. He held up the pink bundle of silk and lace, something frothy and luxurious and absolutely, utterly and diametrically opposed to the role she played in her working hours. It hardly reflected the prim and proper executive assistant who never made a mistake. A woman he called the "Ice Princess" or, on occasion, by her proper name, Carstairs. Typically in a bark.

Though when he said it, it was generally with a slight twist of his nose. As though she smelled bad.

She did not.

"What is this?" he asked.

"That, sir, is my robe."

His lips worked. "I can't wear this—"

"I think it suits you."

"What about the one that comes with the room?"

She nearly snorted. "This is a normal room. We don't get fancy goodies like robes and slippers."

"I didn't ask for slippers."

"Just take it and go. I have plans for tonight."

"Do you?" He had no right to look so petulant. But at least he did as she bade him, pulling the frilly robe on. It barely fit over his muscular arms and most certainly didn't close, but it was fun to look at that incredibly manly man dripping with pink lace.

Well, maybe not fun, *per se*. Because, damn it all anyway, he was still hot.

How was it possible?

He was, without exception, the most aggravating man in existence.

He was hardly the kind of man she wanted, at least in any forever sense. One night might not be bad. In fact, she'd probably fantasized about one night with him. Hard to tell because when his face emerged from the foggy wasteland of her lust, she exiled it.

"Yes," she hissed. "I am going downstairs to party like a wild woman finally free of her bonds."

He seemed oblivious to the sarcasm in her tone. "Surely it can't be that horrendous."

She leaned closer. "My boss is something of a slave driver."

He blinked. "That is horrendous. Why do you work for him?"

Tori opened her mouth to respond, but just then, she realized the stunning and exasperating truth of it.

He had no idea who she was.

Did she really look so different with makeup and a pretty dress that he didn't recognize her? Or was he just that oblivious? Both prospects filled her with a mix of fury and... something else. Something she dared not acknowledge.

The sweet, bitter desire for vengeance though—that she acknowledged.

He didn't have a clue who she was.

Why not have a little fun?

She crossed her arms, knowing what that did to her cleavage, and indeed, his eyes tracked her movements. "He pays well."

"Ah." His Adam's apple worked. "I see." He cleared his throat and met her gaze. "I pay better." A whisper. And it was infused with a seductive timbre. It sent a shiver up her spine. And pissed her off.

Tori sucked in a breath, battling that tangled mix of outrage and lust. "I am not a hooker."

A red tide crawled up his cheeks. "That's not what I was suggesting."

"Really? You have no idea who I am or what I do, yet you are willing to offer me a job? One that doesn't involve *quid pro quo?*"

He had the temerity to look outraged. "I am not that kind of man."

Oh, he was. How many women had left his employ in tears? "It hardly matters. I have no intention of changing jobs." Sad, but true. It was far too much effort to make such a shift, to start over again, and she'd worked damn hard to get where she was.

"Ah, well. There's a pity." He smiled at her. Some charming monstrosity with dimples and sparkling eyes. It was truly horrifying, because it very nearly made her forget everything. Including why it was a terrible idea to tangle with Mr. Savage.

He would chew her up and spit her out.

He would break her heart.

Even worse, if she did as she was so tempted to do, if she seduced him, it would be impossible for them to work together in the future.

It would be a disaster of monumental proportions.

Except... he didn't recognize her.

The temptation grew, tangled, twined with her resolve, pulling it down, deep into the well of her soul, drowning it. She felt the last gasp of it, felt the sad release of its final breath.

Why not?

Why not toy with him? Just for tonight?

Why not take what she wanted from him, rather than the other way around? How delicious would it be to return to her normal life knowing at least some of his secrets? Especially when he had no idea they'd been together?

The prospect was positively scrumptious.

***

"What are you thinking?" he asked, tossing himself into the chair by the window without so much as a how-do-you do.

So like him.

And no! Hell to the no. She was not telling him what she was thinking. Not in a million years. "Why do you ask?"

He shrugged. "Your expression is... "

"Is what?"

That provoking smile returned. "Intriguing."

She huffed. "All right. I was thinking about offering you a drink."

His brow rose. It annoyed her how perfect it was. "Were you? So you're going to let me stay until they come unlock my room?"

"I might." It was important to note that neither of them had suggested calling the front desk, so it might be a while before they came. But she didn't bother mentioning that tidbit. "Would you like a drink?"

"I very much would. But you know what I would like more?"

The heat in his gaze made her a little wobbly. "What?"

"Spending time with you."

Ah.

She'd always suspected this. That he was a man of lethal charm. But she'd never experienced it before. If she was to spend the night—or part of it—with him, she needed to remember that this was only a game. Only a tryst. That there could be no expectation of anything more.

He was a heartbreaker incarnate. She knew it for damn sure. She'd sent a garden full of roses to the bleating women he'd dumped. Racked up thousands of points on her company credit card purchasing diamond parting gifts. She'd spent hours attempting to pacify his weeping castoffs.

He destroyed every woman he touched, if she dared remain close for long.

Surely Tori knew better than to succumb. Surely she could enjoy a few hours with this man without paying for it with her soul.

One night would be enough. It had to be.

Before she could talk herself out of this tantalizing insanity, she said, "What's your poison?"

"Do you have scotch?" he asked.

She didn't have a full bar, like he did in his suite, but she did have a minibar. After a quick scan, she pulled out a tiny bottle of whisky. "Will this do?"

"Perfect."

She nearly jumped out of her skin when he spoke from right behind her; his breath caressed her neck. "Neat?" The word had to be choked out, past the knot in her throat.

"Rocks." God, his voice was sexy like that, all low and rumbly.

She forced herself to step away. "Shall I go get some ice?" She made the offer because he was wearing a frilly pink robe. Not that she wouldn't love for him to be caught by one of his business associates in the hall, but she had other fish to fry at the moment. She could humiliate him later, once she'd had her way with him.

"That would be wonderful."

He watched her as she took the ice bucket to the door. Not that she had eyes in the back of her head, but because she *felt* his perusal. His heat scored her.

She made her way down the hall quickly, probably because her thoughts were racing furiously as well. On the one hand, she knew better than to continue with this course. On the other, she was blinded by what could be.

When she reached the ice machine and noticed that the concierge had returned to his post, she realized that she was at a crossroads. The decision before her was mind-numbing.

She could, with one sentence, end this now.

Or not.

The concierge nodded to her. "Do you need anything, miss?"

The words locked in her throat. She swallowed them down. "I'm fine, thank you," she said, and with it, sealed her fate. Such as it was.

Excitement, hot and seething, whipped through her, making her woozy. She was going to seduce the man who had driven her crazy for three years. She was going to take him and enjoy him and use him as rapaciously as he had used her.

And he was going to like it.

Biting back a wicked smile, clutching her bucket and her resolve to her chest, she hurried to her room. She stopped short to find him still lounging in the chair, but holding her Kindle. Well crap. Why hadn't she thought to hide it? It was full of her secret fantasies and really naughty stories.

He glanced up at her and, *shit*, the expression on his face was horrifying. His wicked lips quirked. The little hairs on her nape prickled. "You read this stuff?"

"Give that back." She stormed over and snatched it from his grip. His grin only widened. He'd stop smiling if she dumped the bucket of ice on him, that was for certain, but before she had time for the thought to manifest, he took the bucket from her and set it on the dresser.

"You are a deeply sensual woman."

"I'm hardly sensual." She was a nerd, first and foremost. He should know. He *paid* her to be a nerd.

"I beg to differ."

"Beg all you want." Yeah, he was her boss, and they were on a business trip, but this was her room. Her own time. She didn't feel the need to play the part of his faithful, invisible minion. Not here at any rate. She whirled on him. "Do you want that drink or not?"

He put his hand to his chest and gave a tiny bow. "I am at your mercy, my lady."

A quote from one of her favorite books, damn it all anyway. She frowned and glanced at her Kindle. "How much of that did you read?"

"Enough." He picked up a glass and filled it with ice. "Do women really want to be ravaged by Highlanders?"

She screwed off the lid to his whisky and filled his glass. "That depends on the Highlander, I imagine."

"I suppose so. Still..."

She glared at him. "Still what?"

"You have a lot of books on that thing. I only scanned one. It makes a man wonder..."

"Wonder what?"

He took a sip of his drink and then gestured to her. "Aren't you having one?"

"Do you often get women drunk to seduce them?"

"Oh. Am I seducing you? I didn't realize. I thought we were having drinks."

Her ire flared, mostly because of his nonchalant tone. She hated nonchalant tones. Especially as foreplay. "You and I both know there's more to this than a few drinks."

Well hell. She shouldn't have been so forthright. His eyes narrowed, his nostrils flared. In that instant he went from being a slightly sarcastic visitor with a drink in his hand to a simmering, beguiling beast.

Though, to be fair to him, he'd always been a beast.

He set his glass on the table and stalked her—no other word for it. Never once breaking his hold on her gaze, he crossed the room and yanked her into his arms. "I am glad to hear it," he said as he lowered his head. And then he kissed her.

It wasn't a sweet and tender thing—but then, she didn't want that.

It was hot and questing and blatant.

And good.

She couldn't stop herself from leaning into him, from encouraging him, from goading him to kiss her more passionately. And he did.

His taste on her tongue, a mixture of whisky and man, was dizzying. The heat of his nearly naked body scorched her. His hands roved, tangled in her wild hair, scudded along her curves, over her pretty frock and down to her flirty skirt.

She shuddered as he reversed his direction and eased up under that skirt.

The feel of his palm, broad and hot, on her ass was scintillating. She held her breath as he traced the band of her panties and then, to her horror and delight, he eased them down. Slowly, so slowly, he brought his hands around to the front and scraped her sensitive flesh with a knuckle.

"What... what are you doing?" she asked, ignoring the wobble in her voice.

He immediately stilled. Pulled back. Met her gaze. "I apologize. I thought this was where we were going."

The thought of him stopping, when he was so close to heaven—when *she* was—made her gut clench. "Well yes, but you're moving pretty quickly." And she wanted him to suffer. She wanted him to ache.

"I cannot help myself. I've never seen such a beautiful woman."

Oh. That infuriated her. Beyond bearing.

Looks were everything to him. All his women were exquisite and perfect and weak.

She was none of those things, and she knew it.

And he did too, whether he recognized her or not.

Without thought, she pushed him away, hard enough that he fell back onto the bed.

Excellent.

She pounced. "This is my room," she said to him, bracing herself on the mattress and hovering over him, staring at him through the curtain of her hair. "I will take the lead."

It was amusing the way his Adam's Apple worked as he gulped. And then he smiled, though it was nowhere near as confident and cocky as it had been a moment ago. He nodded. "Do your worst."

Oh. She would.

She leaned back, sitting on his upper thighs, and surveyed him, considering her options.

He was stunning, lying there on her bed, nearly confined by her robe and nearly exposed as his erection pressed against the slit in his boxers.

How she longed to taste it. Tease it.

"Put your hands over your head." A command.

She was surprised that he complied with such alacrity. She wouldn't have thought him a submissive sort. But then, some men would submit to anything if they thought there might be sex in the offing.

With a sniff to herself at that, she traced the band of his briefs. He flinched, but only when her finger wandered near the entrancing bulge.

"You are hard," she said, teasing the tip.

He huffed a laugh, one twined with panic. "Did you expect otherwise?"

She flattened her palms on his perfect belly and scudded them upward, over his pecs. God, he was hard and warm. His skin was like velvet. "Mmm," she said.

"What's your name?" The question came out in a croak, as though lust had clogged his throat.

She glowered at him. "No names."

"No names?"

"We're just ships, passing in the night."

"Like barges?"

She smacked him. "Just regular ships."

"But I don't know what to call you."

"Make something up."

His lips quirked. "Lusitania?"

"Seriously?"

"Andrea Doria?"

"What?"

"Edmund Fitzgerald?"

She wanted so badly to laugh, but she forced her features into a dour expression. "You cannot name me after shipwrecks."

"Why not?"

"That is hardly a good omen."

"You're probably right. How about I just call you Beautiful?"

She shifted uncomfortably. "I don't like that name either."

"Why?"

"Because I am hardly beautiful."

"You are very beautiful."

"Am not."

"Are too." He pulled her down, onto his chest, and kissed her, probably just to shut her up, it worked.

It did other things too, like raise her blood pressure and make her heart palpitate. God, he was a sexy man. Sexier than any man she'd ever known... when he smiled.

He never smiled at work.

Never.

Not ever.

In three years she'd never seen the like of it.

For some reason, it annoyed her. She shifted up, until she was sitting on his cock. Until he was wedged there, against her tender flesh. He stared at her, and when she began to rock slowly back and forth, his nostrils flared.

She braced her hands on his chest and rode him like a pony, reveling in the scrape of his cock over her clit, reveling in the heat of his body where they connected. She teased him for a while but couldn't withstand it for long, because she was also teasing herself. But his groans were so delicious, she didn't want to stop.

He grabbed her hands in a warm cuff, gentle, but not. "Enough of this," he growled. "I want to fuck you."

Hell yes. She wanted that too. Her mind was awhirl, her body aflame.

"Wait," she said on a sigh.

He froze. "What?"

"A condom. We need a condom." She knew her boss and his profligate ways. This was not happening without protection.

His brow puckered. "Shit. I don't have one."

"You don't?" she asked in a teasing tone.

He huffed a sigh. "I was in my underwear."

Well, that was true.

She smiled at him. "I have one."

"Oh, thank God," he gusted as she scooted off the bed and riffled in her suitcase. It took a minute because, to be honest, it had been a while since she'd needed such an item and she'd forgotten where she'd tucked them.

When she found one, she whirled around and flourished it like a winning Powerball ticket.

"Ah." His eyes glimmered. "You are a perfect woman, aren't you?"

"Working on it." She tossed the condom onto the bedside table and sauntered toward him but he held up one hand, stopping her before she reached the bed.

He flicked a finger at her. "That dress?"

"Yes?"

"It's adorable."

"Thank you."

"Take it off."

His tone scorched her. His intent did too. She folded her fingers and rocked from side to side like an ingénue. It was a ploy to arouse him. She was hardly an innocent. "Take it off?" A steamy pout.

Apparently he had a thing for ingénues. Or resistance. "Take it off. *Now*."

Ooh. She loved the commanding bite of his tone. Maybe because she really wanted to obey. Usually, when he used that tone, she rebelled. Inwardly, at least.

She put out a lip. "But then I'll be naked."

His eyes narrowed. "Off."

With a sigh, she turned her back on him and undid the zipper, but she made it a point to watch his reaction in the mirror. Because it was delicious. He tracked each and every move she made like a feral beast awaiting a banquet.

It was glorious, having his full and complete attention. For once.

The dress fell away, pooling on the floor, and she crossed her arms over her breasts and turned back to him. His attention locked on her panties, a taunting scrap of red lace, and he swallowed. His gaze raked over her bare belly and up to her bra. "Hands to your sides." His voice was raw.

Slowly, she lowered her arms, revealing the matching bra. She made it a point to caress herself, tentatively, teasingly, and was pleased with his reaction.

His lips parted and he breathed one word. "God."

She batted her lashes. "You like?"

In response, he lurched off the bed and grabbed her wrist, yanked her hard against him and cradled her face in his palms. "God." A prayer. And then he kissed her.

It was hard, hungry and raw, a scorching scourge of her lips, an invasion of his tongue.

A madness.

He walked her back to the bed and pressed her down, chest to chest, groin to groin. Everything in her hummed at his nearness. Her nerves awoke and sang. He was glorious and warm and tasted divine. All she wanted was more. More, more, more.

And he gave it to her.

In the flurry of the kiss, his hands roved, finding and cupping her breasts. He grazed her hard nipple with a nail and she groaned as ecstasy danced through her. Then he yanked the lace down and took her with his mouth, sucking, nipping, laving her into a mindless tumult. His other hand skimmed her abdomen, down and down, and she shivered in anticipation as he neared the crux of her thighs, where, at the moment, the entire universe was centered. And throbbing.

When he touched her, softly, reverently, scraping her sanity through the lace, she shuddered.

"Please." She did not intend to beg, but he was killing her. Killing her with his slow, deliberate and agonizing exploration.

"Oh." He lifted his head and shot her a wicked smile. "So you can dish it out, but you can't take it?"

"Fuck you," she snapped, digging her nails into his scalp and pulling him back down to her breast.

She felt his smile against her flesh. "I intend to," he quipped.

God, he was aggravating.

She thrust up her hips and rubbed against his cock. It was hard and full and damp at the tip. "Come on," she urged.

"Not yet," he said, shifting downward. "You're not ready."

Not ready? What the hell did he know about not ready? She opened her mouth to spit some profanity, but before she could think of one appropriate to the situation, he eased down her panties and placed his mouth on her... *and fuck.*

The sensation of that velvet warmth, the nuzzling drag on her aching nub, nearly sent her into the stratosphere. Absolute glory flooded her. She reeled with the impact of her orgasm, but only in the most delicious way. When he slid two thick fingers into her, and he touched *that spot* deep at her core, it took her again.

And oh, he toyed with her, that bastard. Made her come again and again, made her weep, made her writhe and beg. By the time he reached for the condom—with a supremely smug expression on his too-handsome face—she was like a flan, boneless and battered, lying there on the bed barely able to move.

Thank God he left her something, some sprig of energy, because when he levered up and over her and positioned himself at her entrance, she wanted to give as good as she got. She wanted to punish him.

His gaze burned into hers. His breath danced over her cheeks. "Are you ready?" A whisper.

She lifted her knees, dug her fingers into the tight globes of his ass and glared at him, dared him. "Do it."

And he did.

Not soft and gentle. Not slow. Not careful in the least.

He came in hard and deep, taking her more completely than she'd ever been taken, touching her where she'd never been touched. It was magnificent having him in her, tightening on his cock, making him wheeze with pleasure. She never wanted him to withdraw, but thank heaven he did. Because not only did he sink in again with exquisite precision and attention to detail, he did so repeatedly, pummeling her with a dizzying succession of mind-numbing thrusts.

Glorious.

Each plunge pushed her harder, lifted her higher, forcing her closer and closer to that blazing light she knew so well and craved. Maddened and wild, she scored his back with her nails and then, annoyed that he hadn't removed the robe, scored his chest as well. She snarled encouragement into his ear, nipped at his delicious neck and strove to drive him crazy by clutching at him with her internal muscles, until he growled.

His speed increased along with his ragged breath. The sound of flesh slapping flesh rounded the room, twined with their frantic cries as, together, they fought, battled, drove to completion.

She knew when his orgasm was nigh. She felt it in the tension of his body, the fullness of his cock, the tenor of his gasps. She was close too. Too close to stave it off.

But then, she didn't want to. Not really.

When it came, she welcomed it, opened herself to it and him, and succumbed utterly.

It was so sweet, the blossom of that delight. It swelled slowly, rose up and took her ripples of ever increasing intensity. It blinded her, this bliss. Filled her with a sense of well-being and belonging that made her heart tighten and pulsate in her chest.

When it receded, that frenzy, it left her floating on a cloud of supreme contentment.

And him? He collapsed at her side with a sated groan, but he did not cease his nuzzling. As though, like her, he didn't want this to end.

But it had.

And now that it had, now that her lust had been quenched, now that her lunacy of want had been silenced, sanity returned.

He was who he was. She was who she was.

Nothing could *be* between them. Not ever.

And this could never happen again. This would be her secret treasure. A memory he could not share. She simply couldn't allow it.

She stroked his hair, nudging it from his face. "You should go," she said.

He flinched. "So soon?"

"Mmm. I have plans tonight, remember?" She did. She planned to lock herself in this room and blubber for a while. "You gotta go."

"But... I was hoping—"

She pulled herself from his embrace and plodded to her dress and pulled it back on, covering herself, shielding herself. Protecting herself. She forced a smile. "But it was fun," she said in a credible facsimile of a cheerful voice.

"You're really asking me to leave?" He sat up and raked his fingers through his silky hair. His wounded expression made her ache, but she hardened her heart.

"Yes." She turned away so she wouldn't have to see it, walked to the door and opened it. "The concierge is back at his station."

He stood slowly and made his way across the room, stooping to pick up one of her sparkly heels. "You sure?" he asked, stroking the arch of the shoe with a mournful finger.

In response, she waved toward the hall. "Go."

"All right," he said with a glower. "But I'm taking this as a souvenir." And he removed himself from her room, with her favorite shoe in his hot little hand.

She didn't even protest. She didn't have the strength.

She used all she had slamming the door behind him.

***

It was hard getting up the next morning, but she had to.

Still, the alarm on her phone went off three times before she could drag herself out of bed. Every inch ached... but in the most pleasant of ways.

It would be hard facing Mr. Savage today, knowing what she knew now. Knowing that whatever had happened between them, however glorious it had been, wouldn't happen again.

Couldn't.

After she showered, she made an effort to make herself look as dowdy as she'd ever been, hiding herself and her true feelings behind that dull gray suit and those thick glasses. And the heinous bun. When she had completed her disguise, she picked up her briefcase and headed down the hall to Mr. Savage's suite and knocked.

She waited for a while for him to respond, as she usually did. He always made people wait.

She hadn't realized how difficult it would be to tolerate it after last night.

But then lots of things would be difficult to tolerate after last night, she supposed.

And then, when he opened the door and looked at her, a brief dismissive glance, her supposition morphed into a howling certainty.

Yeah. He hadn't recognized her last night. He had no idea he'd spent a rapturous few hours with his frumpy assistant. In fact, he seemed even colder than usual.

"You're late," he clipped, then presented her with his back and returned to the table by the window overlooking the Vegas Strip.

"Sorry," she said, though it was a lie.

"There's coffee and pastries." He nodded to a tray. "Shall we get to work?"

"Yes, sir. But I thought we were leaving today."

He ceased flipping through the papers on the table and frowned at her. "Something has come up. We're not leaving today."

Really? Okay...

"I've been offered an opportunity I want to pursue."

A tiny flame lit in her breast. Could he be talking about... her? Them? Dare she dream?

But then, as she surveyed him, sitting there in his three-piece suit sipping his coffee and re-flicking those poor, abused papers, she had a sudden epiphany.

She didn't *like* this man.

Yes, he was physically attractive and wealthy and successful. But more often than not, he was surly, demanding and driven by ambition. He was cold to the core. He had no sense of humor and the personality of a Vulcan in perpetual *pon farr.*

That was not what she wanted.

Even though she'd seen a side of him last night that she had really enjoyed, one she really wanted to get to know better... there was also this side.

"Carstairs?"

She jerked at his tone as he yanked her from her dark thoughts. "Yes, sir?"

"We have much work to do. Are you ready to begin?"

She was not. "Of course." She reached down and pulled her pad from her briefcase. If she knew Mr. Savage—and she did—they would be here for a while. Hours. She poised her pen over the paper and waited for him to begin.

But deep in her heart, she mourned.

Mourned what could have been, had he been another man.

Mourned the job she once loved, and realized, only now, when it was too late, that she could never stay in his service.

Mostly she mourned the fact that she had allowed herself to do the one thing she'd sworn she would never do.

Fall for him.

Well, not him. Not the man sitting before her with that icy expression and frigid blue eyes.

Her gaze flicked over his face, taking in the details of his beauty. Even the scar over his right eyebrow somehow made him even more—

Her heart stalled. She closed her eyes and tried to remember. He'd had that scar last night, hadn't he?

Of course he had. He had to have. But when she envisioned his face as he took her, when she remembered his cries and his sighs... she couldn't see it there.

How...?

"Is that coffee? I'm parched."

Tori dropped her pen on the carpet but didn't bother to pick it up.

She was far too stunned. She stared at the man who had just emerged from the bathroom. He was dressed in baggy sweats and nothing more, except for a towel looped around his neck. His hair was wet and wild and his body stole her breath.

And he was the spitting image of her boss.

He caught sight of her and grinned. Dimples blossomed. "Well, hello, beautiful," he cooed.

Her jaw dropped. Her gaze raced from this man to Mr. Savage and back. Her mind spun.

Mr. Savage waved in the general direction of the interloper. "Carstairs, this is my brother Max. We'll be working with him for the next several months. You especially."

"Me?" A squeak.

Max grinned. And *damn*.

She knew in an instant, *he* was the one she'd invited into her room last night. He was her wild stallion.

And he wasn't her boss.

Excellent.

Most excellent indeed.

She couldn't hold back her wicked smile. Her heart fluttered when he returned it.

And then, he winked.

7

LIP SERVICE

A Midnight Louie, P.I., Vegas Adventure

Carole Nelson Douglas

If you yearn to be packed with a bunch of strangers like sardines in a tin can, I can recommend no better situation than taking an elevator to the fortieth-something floor of a major Las Vegas Strip hotel-casino.

And the Excelsior Hotel certainly is major. Me? I am content to be taken for a minor player in twenty-first century Las Vegas, when the Strip's Trump Tower has redone the owner's suite in Red, White and Blue. I am not likely to blow my own trumpet, or wear some gravity-defying hair-do.

I am my own best-kept secret and I like it that way. As the unofficial house detective at the Crystal Phoenix, a classy "boutique" hotel-casino, I prefer being overlooked and am uniquely equipped for undercover work. I am the perfect unusual suspect: short, dark and handsome. Really short.

So I am enduring this long elevator ride intending to reach the owner's penthouse, where I am not exactly invited, but what is a little B&E—breaking and entering, as the cops say—between rival hotels?

Although desert temps drop in the evening, Vegas remains mostly hot year round, both as a tourist attraction and a climate, so the odor in the elevator drifting up from open-toed sandals and hothouse laced-up sneakers overwhelms even the sweat-scented reek of underarm deodorants. I understand that ladies need to combat hairy armpits—I suffer from the same problem—but they do not have my same exquisitely powerful sense of smell.

My hearing is extra-sharp as well. I am now detecting the blips of unsuccessfully concealed hiccups. If retching is to follow I am going to exit this swanky ascending sardine can before my goal and take the service elevator, or even the stairs.

Meanwhile, suffering the stomach-churning rhythm of the elevator wafting to a stop at every floor and then lurching upward again, I attempt to identify the hiccupping individual.

Hmm. I home in on a young woman plastered against the elevator's mirrored back wall.

Not bad. Her sandals are high-heeled baby-pink satin on baby-smooth legs as far as I can see. Her sleeveless dress is off-white with iridescent sequins and pearls scattered hither and yon. Her satiny hair is blond, but I cannot detect the color of her eyes since they are squeezed shut. One hand is clapped over her mouth to smother the unfortunate hiccups and the other clutches something at her waist, something that smells sweeter than a happy ending, a natural scent even my jaded nostrils inhale with happy zeal.

Just then the elevator wafts to a stop and the doors open.

"My floor!" Miss Baby Pink manages to mouth between hiccups as she turns sideways to snake her slim figure through parting passengers. "Excuse me, excuse me," she murmurs and almost makes it to the doors when a wrenching sob escapes at last, and at the last possible moment to give her away.

Well, no damsel—or dame, for that matter—in distress shall remain so if Midnight Louie is on hand to offer aid and comfort. I feel through the closing gap, leaving murmurs of disapproval trailing behind me like the train on a bridal gown... or a tail.

As I zip through the closing elevator doors, someone standing right near them whips out with me. The doors close on grumbling riders. I am suddenly in a spacious hall standing cheek by full-figure-calf with the woman who had exited with me.

The fleeing girl is now pacing in front of the opposite bank of elevators. One hand is still covering her mouth and her other is clutched over her midriff as if she is about to have—how can I put it delicately? Well, I cannot. As if she is about to undergo the emergency public evacuation of a hairball, and that would be tragedy for a dainty little doll like her.

"Oh, you poor dear," the portly lady beside me tells her. "All dressed up and trailing tears like rain. How can I help?"

This little doll is indeed lost in her own veil of tears. She had not even noticed we had followed her out of the elevator. She takes in the woman, who holds up empty arms and hands and turns slightly left and then right to further display her harmlessness to the startled girl.

I approve the woman's sensible wardrobe choice. Much more becoming (and useful to me) than the universal, uni-gender Las Vegas choice, Bermuda shorts. Was there ever a garment more fiendishly designed to enlarge the derriere while framing knobby knees like gold leaf surrounding a Picasso painting?

No cursed Bermuda shorts for my new friend. She wears floor-length black palazzo pants, the kind that flare skirt-wide from the knees. As she turns left and right, I follow the fabric flow, cleverly remaining unseen. I sense forthcoming "girl talk" and do not wish to be drawn into such discussions.

Miss Baby Pink blinks at the almost hypnotic sway of fabric.

"What?" Palazzo Pants asks, holding up a barefoot clad in a silver sequined flip-flop, another low-style Vegas icon as popular as Bermuda shorts.

Ordinarily, a guy's guy like me would not be sensitive to female fashions, but I have my reasons for paying close attention to clothing from the knee down.

"What has upset you so?" Palazzo Pants asks.

Miss Baby Pink looks up from the floor. "I thought I saw a... cat, a black cat rubbing on your pant legs."

"Oh, my goodness. I have a cat or four at home, but you are *not* seeing clearly through all those tears."

With Miss Baby Pink distracted, I take the opportunity to survey my impromptu partner in consolation. She is a silver-haired sixty-something with triple bifocal glasses suspended on a sparkly chain around her neck and a large black patent-leather tote bag on her wrist.

"So," this lady asks, "seeing a phantom cat has upset you?"

"No! *Not* seeing something has upset me."

"Was it at a party?" Palazzo Pants nods at the sparkly dress. "Did some cad bother you?"

"Yes! It was at a party. A bridal party. *My* bridal party and the *groom* was some cad who did not 'bother' to show up!" She lifts her left hand from the folds of her full skirt to produce the object she was clutching on the elevator and proceeds to dump it with all her strength into the stainless steel ashtray attached to the marble wall between two elevator cars.

"There! Good riddance to bad rubbish," she says, then takes off at a high-heeled clip down one of the many halls.

My panted friend creeps up on the ashtray as if it might bite.

"What a shame." She lifts something soft and pink trailing curled satin ribbons.

Usually, I cannot resist the flutter of ribbons, the way a gambler cannot pass a spinning roulette wheel, but I ignore them now, straining to identify the article she displays.

"Aaaw," she murmurs. "Clustered candy-pink tea roses with clouds of baby's breath. Such a beautiful bridal bouquet."

She looks around, not looking down. "I cannot bear to see this thrown away."

She thrusts it in the tote bag.

I had not taken her for a bouquet thief. She looks around, then turns with a swish of pants fabric that whips me in the kisser. I follow on her literal heels, sensible canvas flats. Miss Baby Pink has quite a lead on us.

***

Luckily, I am able to match the breathless Palazzo Pants' speed as she storms a hotel room a second before the door closes on her. "Say, darlin' girl, you should not be alone at a time like this. What is your name? Where is your family?"

"I am tired of crying, of being mad or sad every other second." Miss Baby Pink sits on the big hotel sofa, looking like a little girl lost. "My family is at home in Canton, Ohio. They said I was crazy to marry someone I had met so far away from home and so recently."

"Where and when?"

"We met last month on a plane. To Vegas. On *United* Airlines." And she bursts into tears again.

"My name is Corrine Hall," Palazzo Pants says as she ankles over to sit on the sofa, but not too close. Good. I ankle over with her and hunker down under a handy tent of black crepe. I would rather have an ear to the ground than loaf around on a sofa when on the job. And I would rather not be seen *or* heard. I do not bear too much examination. There are some who would question my P.I. credentials, but, at bottom, I am tops at undercover work.

"Amanda," the would-be bride names herself with a sniffle. *"Miss* Amanda Austin."

"Well, Miss Amanda Austin," Corrine says, "tell me all about it. I have been on the marriage-go-round a time or two. Talking it out makes you feel better, and even to see how things really are, or were."

***

It is a tale older than time.

"I fly often for my own business," Amanda begins.

"Your own business! You are the youngest entrepreneur I have ever met!" Corrine waits for more info.

"Nothing big time. I design lines of stationery and greeting cards, both print and online."

"You are shrewd. And creative too."

I can hear Miss Amanda's voice strengthen at Corrine's encouragement.

"Anyway, I travel to trade shows and, of course, Las Vegas hosts trade shows from plumbing fixtures to Ferraris. I always fly economy."

Oh, flying, I think, the tiny aisles, the narrow seats scrunched together. People with their noses buried in "devices". And so irritated and rude. I never take a plane.

"Flying is... both strained and boring these days," Amanda says. "I could afford to upgrade my seat but—"

"But why spend the money?" Corrine interrupted, casting an admiring look at Amanda's full skirt and tiny waistline. "You wear... what? Size zero, and you do not need the legroom."

"Um, I am a size six actually."

"The same as my thigh."

"Corrine, do not put yourself down! You are most attractive. That black crepe outfit is so graceful and flowing—"

All the better to obscure my presence, my dear, I cannot help thinking as I squint my eyes almost shut to take a peek. Alas, my dazzling green peepers (with the iridescent light-reflecting mirrors behind my retinas) can compromise my midnight-black camouflage mode. Luckily, girl talk is totally absorbing to the girls of any age.

"And," Amanda goes on. "Black makes your silver hair look... like a Christmas tree angel's."

All the better to keep your eyes off the floor and me eavesdropping, and on her head, my dear. I am feeling quite... canine, even lupine, about now, listening to Little Pink Riding Hood being gently interrogated.

"Enough about me," Corrine says. "Tell me about *him*."

Amanda frowns. "Why do you think there is a 'him' on this flight?"

"Please," Corrine answers, rolling her eyes.

"All right. I had the window seat of the two, off the aisle. I could not, um, help noticing that the poor man next to me had to put his legs into a 'Z' to fit."

"Well, he might literally have been 'poor.' "Corrine suggests.

"His suit had an expensive sheen, his shirt collar studs looked like gold, and he wore matching cufflinks."

Most intriguing, think I. The dude indeed was wearing high-end duds for economy class. Miss Amanda is one observant little doll.

"Hmm. Dark and handsome as well as tall, I bet," Corrine purrs as Miss Amanda blushes. "What about his tie?"

"Navy blue silk, to match his eyes."

"How would you see his eyes, if they were focused only on a tablet or phone screen, like everybody else on the plane?

"I always do the airline magazine crossword puzzle, and he could not help seeing it. He prompted me on an answer because he had solved it on a previous flight."

"Now, I would find that nosy and annoying, Amanda. The nerve!"

"He needed *some* distraction from that awful pretzel position."

"And you think a crossword puzzle was more interesting than you?"

"Well, we both love them, and he got up a fresh one his cell phone to solve together."

"Hmm." Corrine obviously joined me in picturing Miss Amanda's blond head together with that of Mr. Tall, Dark, Handsome and Pretzeled.

As Amanda prattles away, I tote up my private investigator conclusions. The couple had fallen for each other at first sight. They had so much in common, Amanda said, but they lived on opposite coasts, so they emailed and tweeted and Skyped after the flight.

My ears perk up when she says they had a big bond. She had a Shih Tzu, he had a Rhodesian Ridgeback.

(I translated that to mean she had a sneeze and he had some sort of collectible foreign coin.)

"*Ooh*, dog lovers," Miss Corrine coos. "One so tiny and one so big. The dogs, I mean. A perfect match." It takes all kinds. I am *not* a dog lover.

They planned to wed and honeymoon in Vegas. All her girlfriends and family mocked her impulsive feelings. She defied them, but then he did not show up. So humiliating. The Excelsior wedding chapel people said cases like hers were why they required pre-payments.

They let her keep the bouquet, gratis.

She would *never, ever* forgive him if she ever saw him again, which she would not.

"An emergency could have prevented him from coming," Corrine suggests.

Amanda waves the oversize cell phone from her petite pink satin purse that matches her dress and shoes. Even I have to admit, despite her red nose and eye-whites, she makes a beautiful bride.

Corrine draws her own cell phone from her tote bag like a weapon. "What is his name?"

"I never want to hear or say it again!"

"Just long enough for me to see if he booked a room."

"I tried that first. They said no."

"Name?"

Amanda sighed. "Kyle."

"K-y-l-e. First or last?"

"First."

"Last name."

Amanda hesitates. "Adams. I know, it sounds so bland. So fake."

Corrine was already talking to the front desk. "Will you check again? Thanks."

Amanda taps a pink satin toe on the carpeting while we wait.

"I see." Corrine's frown lines deepen. "Wait. Try Adam Kyle." She covers the receiver and whispers to Amanda, "They could have listed surname first." Her attention returns to the speaker, and then her thin, arched eyebrows lift. "Yes! The room was cancelled... when? Last night."

Amanda is not encouraged. "That is just fine. Mr. Adam Kyle or Kyle Adams is cancelled out of my life. I am checking out tomorrow."

"Do you not have any attendants here?"

"I told you. Anyone I would have asked thought I was crazy. Kyle and I, or Adam and I, were going to stay on for two nights as a honeymoon. *I* am cancelling my room too. May Kyle and Adam be very happy together. I am going home tomorrow morning."

"Do not give up on your vanished Prince Charming. I still think something beyond his control happened. Someone on the front desk may have a clue." Corrine stands. "I will report back."

Amanda stands too. "You are very kind, Corrine. I am not ordinarily this impetuous, but even if he can be found and provide some excuse, he can just join that bridal bouquet in the hotel Dumpster."

"*Tsk. tsk.* I will be back in an hour or two with some answers. I hope."

Whither Corrine and her palazzo pants go, I goeth, so I am soon lurking in the hall outside room 47 come 11, as they sort of say in craps.

I wistfully watch Corrine's pant legs swish down the hall. I am here on serious business and must get up to the penthouse suite as soon as possible. I will race after Miss Corrine and resume my journey upward.

My main mission regards my role as house detective at the Crystal Phoenix Hotel and Casino, so I must visit the more than somewhat shady owner of the Excelsior, Louis "The Lip" LaFica. (No relation, thank Bast. *I* keep *my* lips zipped.)

***

Once I slip onto an elevator with Miss Corrine, I am on the Easy Entry Express. Vegas hotels slather dark, splashy-patterned carpet on every horizontal surface to hide stains from spilled food or drink. My signature Basic Black coat fades right into the flooring. As long as I keep moving to avoid being inadvertently stepped upon, I am an easy rider. When the last person in my car has reached his floor, forty-three, and exited, I jump up to hit the Open Door button, then leap up much higher to swat the panel button for the fiftieth floor, which does not house any guests because no one would want to visit there.

It is the penthouse floor, the home and business operations headquarters for Louis the Lip himself.

Yes, that high a number is a mighty leap even for one of my muscular, if height-disadvantaged, frame. It takes several jumps to punch that button down enough to stay depressed, but the journey resumes with a tiny hiccup. Soon the doors open, with me crouched on the side opposite the controls.

Confronting an open elevator, people always look for the control panel first.

I expect to confront a wise guy in an Armani suit wearing a Glock semiautomatic like a glove, but not two of them. I barely slither myself around the open door into the room beyond before those size eleven, brown, oxford wing-tips are stomping all over the elevator carpet.

Luckily, the penthouse floor sports a wide black marble border. It is a trifle cold on the bare tootsies and tummy, but I belly-crawl like a commando under barbed wire along the main room's edges, silent and unseen.

The penthouse lair of Louis "The Lip" LaFica is not only reputed to be luxurious, but safe from storming by other mobsters or the FBI, and also useful as a launching pad to *The Long Concrete Goodbye* for anyone The Lip might take a disliking to.

Right now Louis has his immediate "Muscle" gathered around a computer on his massive mahogany desk, and his Lip around a huge stinky cigar that may be expensive, but still qualifies for the expression "wolf turd".

"The elevator was empty, Boss," a guy yells from beside my former container.

"Those tourists," Louis the Lip comments. "Cannot even get lucky hitting the right floor." All the boys guffaw on cue. "Not at the Excelsior," one adds.

"Shuddap," The Lip snarls. "The Trumpster just tweeted the Excelsior is fifty stories shy of class. I gotta answer back: @OldMcDonaldTrumpWearsBangs. 'Yeah, and your Trump Tower needs a new toupée'."

Louis the Lip checks his watch, a Rolex so overloaded with features he can only lift his arm as high as his belt. He squints at the clock hands hidden amid the gold, platinum, and rose gold dials and whistles.

"About now our army of 'excluded persons' and 'advantaged players' are fanning out over the Crystal Phoenix gaming area. These card counters and cheaters will wipe the coffers dry before the Fontana brothers can lift a finger. They will lose millions. That will teach their uncle Macho Mario Fontana he is just an old wimp. Imagine him calling me 'a has-been cheap thug the real Mob would not use to mop the Excelsior men's room'."

"That reminds me, Boss," a lackey says, "what do we do about the guy we caught checking out our own gaming area and stashed in the executive bathroom? The one who says he just came here to get married?"

"Nobody comes to the Excelsior just for that." The Lip removes the giant stogy from his big fat mouth and regards the burning end. "Let us light up and amble in for a friendly chat."

Louis the Lip's toadies all pull out cigars of the same classless size, producing a sinister ring of burning embers. It is all I can do not to choke and sneeze amid the fumes.

Thanks to all that smoke swirling around their heads, though, and the fact that all the rooms in this place are bordered with black marble, I can pad silently and unseen after them to this "executive bathroom" place. I imagine it will be as tastelessly lavish as The Lip's office.

Am I wrong. I stand shocked to the hairs of my chinny chin-chin. The place is like an operating room, walls, ceiling, floor all covered in shiny white tiles, with a big rusty drain in the middle. Uh, that would be 'bloody', I guess. I am drawn forward for a closer look. A nice-looking young guy in a navy blue suit with a red carnation in the lapel is tied to a Lucite armchair in the classic position, with white ropes around his ankles and binding his wrists to the chair arms.

I am pleased the poor guy's gagged head lolls forward, unconscious. All the mobsters inhale deep on their cigars and exhale a blue fog.

"Let us soften him up for a few more hours, then we will give the groom-to-be the stag party of his life," Louis the Lip says with an evil chuckle.

I am so shocked that I forget for a moment I am standing on white tiles and would look like a giant tarantula against this "operating room" floor as the crooks turn to leave their chamber of horrors. I scoot behind the commode, a sinister model in black porcelain, until I can follow the last goodfella out and blend with the black marble ringing the outer room. First, I insert my muscular rear member in the door before it is quite closed. And a welcome distraction shows up just then.

The elevators open to disgorge a gorgeous woman in a white nurse's outfit of the old school, the kind used from time to time in certain scenarios at Nevada's famous legal brothels.

The goodfellas gather around the dame, so thick I can descend in the empty elevator with as much notice as a cockroach. I must get Mr. Kyle out of danger, but first I must alert someone to act as a go-between.

Okay. I am of two minds. It is clear I need to be in two places at once.

And, although I am very good at a lot of things, astral projection is not one of them. I must get Miss Amanda's fiancée out of there pronto. First, I must ensure my little doll does not leave the building. Elvis can, whenever he likes. And, believe me, I have personal knowledge that he has *not* left the Strip. But Miss Amanda must be persuaded to remain until she meets up with a freed Kyle and I have accomplished my mission to foil Louis the Lip's scheme to bankrupt the Crystal Phoenix.

***

Hotel service carts covered in white linen make a fine tent for me. I hitch a ride with the penthouse luncheon dishes to the back service elevator, able to munch on shrimp scampi and chicken Caesar salad. Sadly, there are no half-bloody steak or buttered lobster leavings. Apparently the mob is on a diet or watching its high cholesterol. They are a graying population now.

I am wheeled into the elevator and down to the hotel kitchens, where I often visit on vermin patrol and to supervise the menu at the Crystal Phoenix. I am head seafood taster and check out every flake that falls. I have never met a substandard fish there, so I can heartily recommend the restaurants to all and sundry and all the little sundrys. (The Phoenix is a family-friendly establishment, unlike the Excelsior which specializes in all the vices Vegas is famed for, including assignations not requiring the prop of a bridal bouquet.)

The happy sight of delivery carts lined up to be filled with piping hot food has me applauding my next move. Taped-on order forms show the room number written large, also the guest's last name. Oh, happy coddled cods! Three carts are destined for the forty-seventh floor. And the order info on one of them has possibilities for a dude like me not above a bit of duplicity and digital manipulation, and by digital manipulation I am not talking opposable thumbs, which I lack.

It is a good thing I was deposited in a library return slot as a babe. It made quite the news. ATROCITY AMONG THE DEWEY DECIMAL SYSTEM SET: ABANDONED BLACK KITTEN DUMPED. Heck, I had hopped in there myself to get out of the hot sun. It is true my Ma was a homeless street person, so we all had to go it alone pretty young. Anyway, the lady librarians cooed over me and named me Baby Dewey and let me sleep my way through several sections of books with a sandbox to play in and donations of canned fish from library patrons. When I opted to explore the larger world, I had learned my ABZs, so to speak, and had a degree in ZZZing.

Anyway, one customer of a fancy cart heading to the forty-seventh floor is named—thank Bast!—Carlyle. It takes but a Zorro slash or three with my hidden shivs to make "Car" into a nice big—okay, messy but legible—capital K. Thank you, head librarian Miss Jane McBain. As for the room number, a scrawled 4722 is a snap to make 4711 with straight shiv slashes though the last two numbers.

I leap onto the cart's lower shelf as the tablecloth falls shut behind me and big shoes surmounted by white pants surround me. Soon I am rattling and rolling over tiles into the service elevator. In no time we are speeding over hall carpeting and come to a stop with a smart half-circle turn. I hear the waiter knock. I listen with bated breath. Did the staff take my bait?

Rats! I hear another party approaching fast from the direction of the guest elevators.

The door opens.

"Yes?" Miss Amanda asks from behind the chain lock. Smart girl. You never know who may be lurking outside your door at a hotel. Like... me!

"There must be some mistake," Miss Amanda says. "I did not order—

"This is Room forty-seven-eleven," the waiter says.

"Yes, but... "

"What is the problem?" a new but not-new-to-me voice asks.

"Corrine." Miss Amanda sounds relieved. "I am afraid there has been a mistake. I did *not* order from room service."

"Who did?" Miss Corrine is not a lady to fool with.

I hear the rustle of my doctored label. "Written kinda fast," the waiter says. "Like hen scratches, ma'am. I would say... K-something."

A gasp from inside the door and then from outside it.

"Kyle?" Corrine asks.

"Sure. That is the name!" says the waiter. "You want it or not?"

"No!" says Miss Amanda inside.

"Yes!" says Miss Corrine in the hall. "Of course we want it. We just did not expect Kyle to do anything so... lavish."

So she has spotted the champagne bottle and red roses in a vase among the stainless-steel covered dishes. When Midnight Louie hijacks a room service cart, he does not go cheap. Nor should Mr. Kyle at this point.

So I am wheeled in with dispatch, unbeknownst to all. As the waiter begins to set up the champagne and unveil the dinner, I untangle myself from the bottle stand to hide behind the bed's dust ruffle. As I make my move, my second most valuable member happens to brush the waiter's hand.

"A feather duster," he mutters. "Housekeeping is getting careless." He straightens, grinning, to deploy the cart's contents on the desk.

Meanwhile, Miss Corrine is hissing discreetly at Miss Amanda. "The tip, and make it good."

"I will not," she whispers back. "I am not to be bought off with champagne and roses."

"Then you are a crazy woman." Miss Corrine's voice returns to speaking level. "Thank you."

"Thank *you*, ma'am." A happy, well-tipped waiter departs and Miss Amanda goes to slide the safety latch closed after him.

She turns with her back braced against the door, as if trapped inside with something scary.

Corrine is admiring the champagne label. "Good year." She lifts a stainless lid. "Filet mignon for two, Caesar salad, truffled mashed potatoes, baked Alaska for dessert. Kyle did not spare the bucks."

"Face it. It is a mistake, Corrine," Miss Amanda says.

"K as in Kyle," Corrine sing-songs, pouring a flute of champagne.

"That is a first name, not a last name. Who orders that way?"

"We were not sure about that, remember?"

"I do remember, Corrine, and whether the man is Kyle Adams or Adam Kyle, he stood me up after sweeping me off my feet."

"Sounds kind of gallant," Corrine says. "At least he got you upright again."

"You know what I mean. He is not even registered at this hotel."

"No, he is not. Although the night desk clerk was coming on duty and recognized my description of him."

"What description?" Amanda snapped. "Tall, dark, and handsome?"

"Of course, but I believe you also said piercing dark blue eyes."

"I would never describe eyes as 'piercing'."

"Well, the night desk clerk sure would, and she said he arrived at three this morning, but can find no record of him registering."

"She said that?"

"That there was no record of her checking him in? Yes."

"I mean," Miss Amanda said, crossing her arms over her chest, and incidentally, her heart, "she said that he had 'piercing blue eyes'. That proves he is a heartless flirt."

"That proves he is attractive." Corrine shrugged. "What? You wanted to marry the hunchback of Notre Dame?"

"Maybe, if he came swinging down on his bell rope on time, not leaving me looking like a fool at the hotel wedding chapel."

"The desk clerk did not report a disability, but she *did* mention he had a cleft chin like Cary Grant."

"Yes, that is Kyle! But he is not here."

Obviously, the man must be held up somewhere. He called ahead to order this private after-wedding dinner for two."

"But how would he know what room I was in?

"He used your name and the hotel knew where they put *you*, for heaven's sake."

"But they misplaced *him*?" Amanda sat on the desk chair, eying the sparkling crystal and silverware. "It does look like he ordered all this and now... would be, would be—" Her fist stopped another fit of tears. "Would be the exact time when we would be coming up to the room after the ceremony. You are right, Corrine. Something stopped him from going to his own wedding! How can we find out what?"

"I hate to let this swell dinner go to waste, but we need to cross-examine the desk clerk further. Fix your face and we will get on the trail."

I hear and see the patter of feminine feet trotting back and forth before they head for the door, me on the heels of Miss Corrine's positively shimmying pant legs.

Waiting for the elevator, while I hunch in a rather funereal tent of black crepe, Miss Amanda continues to ponder. "Maybe I was too hasty to judge. Kyle could have fallen ill in his room, been knocked out robbed there, even!"

"Excellent idea, Amanda."

"To be robbed in one's room?"

"To suggest that to the hotel management so they get working on finding where he went and why the check-in failed to show up in the computer but the cancellation did."

I dance inside the arriving elevator again, careful to avoid any brushes against Miss Corrine's lower legs. In the car people come and go, while I crouch in my unlighted corner, waiting for the last rider to leave the highest floor before I perform my perfected leap-and-punch routine to get to the penthouse.

Now for the hard part.

***

Getting back into The Lip's lair is easy. His goons are coming in one by one, reporting on the deployment of every blacklisted cheating player in Vegas at work throughout the Crystal Phoenix casino. My hair is bristling like a radiator brush. They are so busy high-fiving each other and drinking champagne that I slip into the sinister bathroom unseen.

Mr. Kyle makes a slight groan as I enter, and I see a glimmer of blue between his almost closed eyelids. No way would I describe his gaze as "piercing" or even alert now. I knock on one of his kneecaps, shivs halfway deployed, to waken him.

"Sssss," I hiss when he sees me. I look to the door, open only the width of my no-longer sleek mid-section. The late hours a detective works messes with my fat-burning metabolism, I am sad to say.

He listens to the congratulatory hullabaloo in the outer office, describing every crooked rip-off going down at the Phoenix.

Mr. Kyle is fully conscious now. He takes action by pushing at me with his shoes, trying to kick me!

What an ingrate! I pull back. Wait. He is using one heel to push the shoe heel off his other foot. He is wearing black slip-on loafers in a slick Italian style one might spot in a less morbid color on one of the famous Phoenix Fontana brothers. The shoe is off but an odor of hot black sock assaults my nostrils. For an instant, I am tempted to let Kyle face his fate unaided. I am no bloodhound, but my sense of smell is fine-tuned. Being of short stature, I suffer much from foot-odor fumes in a hot climate like Nevada's.

Mr. Kyle has not noticed my semi-swoon and is trying to insert his toe in the shoe again. What the foot? Ah. Given the grimly determined look on his face, he is not simply undoing his latest move. I none too gently shiv his foot arch right through the abominable sock. He pulls away, smothering a naughty word in his gag, while I work my own clever tootsies into the shoe's toe and in no time pry out... a cell phone. A small plastic-protected cell phone with a set of numbers ready to dial.

There may have been a time, in the Good Old Days of hard-boiled private detectives when one of my ilk would have been reduced to knocking a black phone receiver off of a bulky black cradle, or perhaps, more recently, paw down a button on an answering machine. But it is all cell phones these days, even though service can be iffy in the technological buzz generated by Las Vegas's over-electrified, power-sucking needs. But I know enough—and my compact twenty pounds are heavy enough—for my right forepaw, shivs in, to press the pretty green illuminated image (like my eyes at night) of an old-fashioned telephone receiver and make an up-to-the minute rescue call.

A man's voice answers immediately. "Kyle? We have been waiting for your call. Got our hands full here. Where are you? Kyle?"

Aha! Kyle is a Vegas P.I. the Fontanas hired to stop a suspected scam. He was probably following someone in economy for another case when Miss Amanda met him on that plane.

Now, gagged, Kyle can only make muffled noises. I add a cry or two in my native Bast, but the raucous shouted rejoicing from the outer office wafts into the bathroom and echoes loudly.

"The Phoenix is cooked!"

"Naw, Boss, the Phoenix is 'crooked' to the max!"

"No one there will ever call Louis the Lip a cheap thug again," The Lip yells, "because they will not be in business any more."

***

Meanwhile, I saw away with tooth and nail at Mr. Kyle's wrist ropes, uninterrupted. Men still enter to join the rowdy yelling in the office. When the bathroom door slams open, I hightail it behind the commode and hope the thugs will not notice the shredded wrist ropes or the tell-tale cell phone on the floor, although Mr. Kyle managed to get his foot back in his shoe, which makes my nose rejoice.

Then we are really swarmed by gangsters, gangsters in ice-cream color designer suits. Think Pierce Brosnan clones if he had been Italian. The Fontanas are indeed a large Italian family, with ten, sharp, sleek Fontana brothers-about-town, only two of them married, which it looks like Mr. Kyle might soon be, as he is released and pounded on the back.

All he can say is, "Amanda. Is Amanda all right?"

"Only crooks and cops are here. And us Fontanas."

Who sort of meet in the middle of that combo, think I.

By then they are out in the main office, where other brothers are discreetly assisting uniformed officers rounding up Louis "The Lip" LaFica and his crew, who stink of cigars and splashed champagne.

I, of course, am overlooked as usual, and as usual, like it that way, except that I am a bit miffed this time. My diversion with the room service dinner was genius. Not to mention the cell phone deduction and usage. I did all but talk. Which I refuse to do with inferior species on principle.

"Good job, Adams," Aldo is crowing. "Ingenious to go undercover as a wedding chapel customer."

"Tell me they do not have Amanda."

"Uh," Aldo asks, "who is Amanda? Another operative?"

"My bride," Kyle says with a groan. "If she is still in Vegas. The wedding was real. She wanted to do it here for some reason. I never considered they might nab me checking out the assembling shysters in their casino practice run for the Crystal Phoenix scam. What will I do? Amanda probably assumes I stood her up, and is upset."

You think?

Well, they at least think to check the hotel desk, and Kyle, accompanied by five Fontana brothers to verify his story, is soon hurrying to Room 4711, still occupied. And, if I am right, should remain so for the night. No need for me to go and see for myself. I am a dude of action, but not an onlooker of same.

***

The next day, the wedding chapel at the Crystal Phoenix is a fairyland of shining, faintly tinkling crystal chandeliers and fountain,s and a bower of exotic flowers and greenery. Miss Corrine Hall is

Matron of Honor and hotelier Nicky Fontana himself is best man. The service was touching and the couple will have three days and nights in the Bridal Suite. The groom is handsome in a new gray suit of Fontana quality and his lucky wedding shoes. The bride wears the charming street-length, delicately glittering dress she had bought far from Las Vegas and planned on, despite offers of a new wedding and honeymoon wardrobe. She carries a simple, small bouquet of tightly clustered tea roses and baby's breath.

I too, am a witness, a silent witness, hidden among the bright green pots of ferns, which match my eyes, although nobody notices, and that is the idea.

Yet, I am a detective, and, after the champagne reception and congratulations—to the couple and among the Crystal Phoenix folk for outfoxing Louis the Lip—I discreetly follow the young couple to the elevators. I do take credit for the happy ending, after all.

Rare for Las Vegas, the space before the elevators is empty, and Mr. and Mrs. Kyle Adams repeat the ceremonial kiss, longer and deeper and with feeling. I look away, embarrassed. I mean, my species gets the tongue bit, but really…

The last I see is their backs disappearing, arm in arm, like the couple atop a wedding cake, into the elevator car.

And in the cigarette tray affixed to the marble wall—a most tasteful chrome and crystal bowl, mind you—lies a perfect little wedding bouquet. Some might consider it abandoned, but I believe it was left as a gift.

Who will find it? I wonder. Will someone rescue it? Who left it at the Excelsior in the first place? Why did Miss Corinne keep the first bouquet, as a memento of an untold story of her own? There are forty million tourist stories annually in the entertainment capital of the world called Las Vegas. This has been just one of them, but I have at least one thousand and one more.

8

CRIME BEFORE LOVE

Kathryn Falk, Lady of Barrow
with
Carolyn Haven and Chantelle Aimée Osman

Carla Lightfoot stepped out of the taxi a block from the Palermo restaurant in Carroll Gardens, voted "the place most likely to see, and be seen by, the Mafia" according to *New York Magazine*. Her vintage Hermès boots splashed through the puddles and light Brooklyn rain. Under the familiar red and green canopy she took out a mirror to straighten her hair, check her makeup and see if anyone was tailing her. The street was quiet tonight.

She could smell the wafting of basil, almost taste the veal meatballs with just the right amount of seasonings, and imagine the dribble of fresh roasted tomato sauce kissing her lips as she pushed open the stained glass double doors. An imposing, pinstriped figure stood at the top of the staircase leading to the private dining room.

"Come, give your uncle a hug," he called out.

She handed her damp things to the maitre'd and hurried up the steps to fold him in a tight embrace.

"So, what's this meeting all about?" She couldn't help but be curious, mid-week was outside of routine. More like business.

He gave her a cryptic smile. "I had a call from Giovanni, seems there's some problems at the Excelsior in Vegas. But don't worry about it now. Come, eat."

Carla was a loyal niece. Even though she had been at junior college in San Antonio, near her mother and stepfather, she had visited her uncle Paul regularly while he served three years in the Brooklyn

House of Detention for tax evasion. Paul had a brilliant flair for analyzing games of chance, and ran the most successful bookmaking operation in New York. "Math and gambling are intertwined," he'd remind her every time they went to the track.

While inside, he asked her to read the latest copies of *PC Magazine* and *Popular Science* and keep him up to date. As a result, she developed a passion for computers and chose to specialize in cybersecurity after receiving her undergraduate degree in Informational Technologies.

Carlo—the legend she learned was her father on her sixteenth birthday—had never been to prison. He wanted his family to own legitimate businesses and be successful professionals, and Carlo was proud that his brother had encouraged his daughter to embrace new technology. Carla was part of the clean branch of the family. She went on to earn her master's degree from NYU, where she settled to be near her extended family, then was recruited by the Department of Homeland Security.

"Does the DHS know you're here?" asked Uncle Paul.

"*I* didn't tell them," she winked and walked through the doors and into the private room.

Before sitting down, Carla removed a small black box with two antennas from her leather tote. She put her finger to her lips in a silent signal to the group not to speak.

"This detects wireless protocols." At everyone's blank stare, she clarified, "Bugs, it detects extra fancy bugs."

She had spent her school holidays working for the family at the Excelsior Resort and Casino in Las Vegas and earned the respect everyone showed her by overseeing the software for the family's elite, luxury property.

"But I need your phones off... yes, the burners too." Carla was charming and clever like her mother, but had the personality of her late father—cautiously confident and quietly ruthless.

Phones came out and beeped as they were powered down. Carla scanned the room as quickly as possible, then ran the device over everyone seated at the table. The device remained silent, and Carla nodded at her uncle.

The waiters brought out a sumptuous feast with Chianti, served family-style. Carla caught up with all her relatives and enjoyed fish, pasta, and her favorite: fried zucchini.

"Now to business," Uncle Paul announced after finishing his espresso and the room was sated. "Our resort in Vegas is vulnerable to cyberattack. I don't want us to be taken advantage of. Obviously, we are not calling in the police when we can do it ourselves." He motioned to Carla then continued. "The Excelsior hasn't been hit hard... *yet*. But several nearby hotels have, and it's only a matter of time. We need someone to update the systems, assess the at-risk areas, and develop new protocols as soon as possible. Our clientele is elite—and paranoid."

Everyone at the table murmured, digesting the information with the same relish they had finished off the desert. Slowly, every head turned to Carla, who smiled and stood.

"Well, of course I'll help." Carla loved her job with Homeland Security but family was sacrosanct. "I can take a leave from work. I haven't taken a vacation in years, and I know they don't want to lose me."

The DHS office on Court Street in Brooklyn was where she spent most of her days—and an overlarge portion of her nights—had benefited from both her skills and the connections her family provided.

"I don't see the DHS having a problem, they may even want me to do it on their dime. They've been monitoring these same incidents. Last year, 250 Hyatts were compromised worldwide and the hackers stole thousands of credit cards, not to mention the theft of passports and valuables from safes. Ditto for Marriotts and Hiltons. The hackers seem to have switched from box stores to the hospitality industry, because the fruit hangs low."

"Speaking of low hanging fruit," chimed in her older cousin Anthony, "I'm confirming the rumor Uncle Giovanni asked me to look into about a fence who's moving high-ends goods out of Vegas."

She chided, "You know I don't want to hear that. You can tell Giovanni that news yourself when you call him on Sunday."

Don Paul laughed and hugged her. "As my big brother used to say, 'You have to be like a lion and a fox. The fox is smart enough to recognize traps, and the lion is strong enough to scare away the wolves.'" He looked her in the eye. "Be like a lion and a fox, niece, and no one will ever beat you. Stay safe."

***

It had been almost *too* easy to get approval for her leave of absence from the DHS. If she didn't know better she'd think something was up with those G-men, but then, it usually was.

When her flight landed, she followed the resort's chauffeur to the Excelsior's black limousine. As the bright lights of her youthful stomping grounds came into sight, her excitement grew. Vegas was gaudier than New York, like Times Square on acid, without question, but she loved it. Carla hoped she wouldn't have to constantly be chained to the computer rooms for the next two months.

"Welcome back, Ms. Lightfoot," the Excelsior doorman bowed and saw to her luggage. The grand European style lobby surrounded Carla in welcoming warmth. Light from the Murano glass chandeliers reflected off the gold leaf accented ceilings, shimmering above lavish carpeting and elegantly upholstered furniture. She walked through a set of frosted glass doors to be hit by the familiar noises of a crowded casino. The one-armed bandits were in a separate section, so as not to distract the distinguished high rollers playing baccarat, poker, blackjack and roulette. She took it all in, but spared a skyward glance to the faces behind the cameras overhead. A quick visit to the tech department made Carla realize this project would take longer than everyone expected.

***

With Carla's help—and that of a few MIT grads she pulled in—the Excelsior's in-house technology teams made significant improvements in a few short weeks. Their big Valentine's Day party would be a test run for the new systems as well as for networking with their partner hotel, the Rio. Giovanni wanted to show the Badolatos what needed to be done to protect both resorts. It was a longstanding relationship her family had fostered in 1960 when they invested in the Excelsior.

"Vincent Badolato is coming to the party. Alone." Her uncle had not-so-subtly informed her with a waggle of his eyebrows when the first round of RSVPs had come in. She had given him an over-exaggerated, teenage eye roll for his matchmaking efforts. He sighed. "You don't date; you have no boyfriend. And don't think I haven't noticed. Vincent has grown into a fine man. He runs the Rio now. He would be good for you."

Truth be told, as a teen, she had crushed hard on the handsome soccer player, but never acted on her feelings. Always working hard and focused on school, she didn't have time for relationships. So, she had let him steal a few kisses, but never anything more.

Her uncle's information had nothing whatsoever to do with the low-cut red Vera Wang cocktail dress she wore that night that set off her shoulder-length blond hair and her Cherokee mother's slim figure—she just enjoyed looking sexy.

More nervous than she admitted over the prospect of seeing Vincent, she made her rounds, stopping to chat with a few people from the old days. She excused herself from the recently hired concierge for the Excelsior, Alexander Braillowski, a dapper-looking man with prematurely gray hair and a habit of standing way too close when he conversed. She hated hair gel—it reminded her of the wanna-be criminals in Little Italy. Despite the fact that he wore Les Clefs d'Or, the concierge symbol of excellence, he sent up all sorts of red flags for her.

After the awkward encounter, Carla needed a drink. Heading to the bar, she was surprised to see Matthew Mulligan, a DHS agent from the Houston office, artfully twirling a bottle. Apparently, the DHS was making their move and hadn't deigned to inform her. She'd known Matt since her NYU days. He was thoughtful, handsome and smart— an amusing friend. Their time spent in bed was no more than a convenience for her, despite his repeated attempts to make it serious.

She sidled up to the bar, and just loud enough to be heard, commanded, "Make me a Mudslide, and it had better taste damn good or you're fired. This is *my* hotel."

Matt's eyes rounded in surprise for a split second—he may not have been expecting her either— before he began juggling two bottles. His seductive smile and blue eyes put Tom Cruise in *Cocktail* to shame. Of course, his uniform of a black leather vest and no shirt drew enough attention on its own. Judging by the stack of telephone numbers and tips in his jar, his cup runneth over.

"When did you get here?" he whispered, sliding her drink over on an Excelsior coaster. "After you try this, you'll want to give me a raise."

Carla sipped the creamy, chocolate drink, and winked at him. "You can stay, but without a heads up, I'll have to think about that raise."

"Glad to hear it, Boss. It's my first day."

Before Carla could comment, he was halfway down the bar, taking an order from another familiar face, Madam Ann, owner of the top escort service in Vegas and an organizer of "Hookers 4 Hillary". Carla sipped the drink, surveying the crowd for a few quiet moments before turning toward the room at large. Someone bumped her elbow. Fortunately, what was left of her Mudslide sloshed safely inside the glass rather than on her dress.

"Excuse me," she preemptively said to the party goer, setting her drink on the bar.

"Carla, Carla Lightfoot? It's me, Natalie Logan! We went to high school together in San Antonio. I was a year behind you. We competed in the National Computer Applications Competition. You won in the tiebreaker."

"Oh, Natalie. Hi! It's good to see you. What are you doing here?" Carla's mind worked furiously trying to place the statuesque brunette.

"My aunt passed away and I inherited her flower shop. We've expanded beyond weddings and high school proms—we're a part of hospitality services at the Excelsior now," she finished proudly.

"Did you do the beautiful arrangements for tonight?" She recalled her uncle mentioning contracting a new florist. "They smell heavenly."

"They were flown in from Ecuador just for this event. Only the best for our clients."

"I'm curious, have you had any problems with credit card theft?"

"No, knock on wood. I've still got enough skills to keep my business safe." Natalie removed a business card from her silver card case and passed it to Carla. "You know, if you're going to be in Vegas a while, we should get together and catch up."

There was something more than training holding Carla back from readily accepting the invitation.

"That would be great, if I can get away."

"Well, if you find the time, you have my number." Turning away, she smiled at Carla, but it didn't reach her eyes.

Carla watched the woman walk gracefully across the carpet on four-inch heels. Heads turned as she crossed the room, Vincent Badolato's among them.

He'd grown up, filled out and looked sexy as hell in an open-neck shirt, white blazer and bespoke trousers. Carla's girlhood crush flared and sprouted wings. She felt the moment Vincent saw her—he stopped talking, the tension grew palpable. The look he gave her was far more intimate than he'd earned. A blush almost as red as her dress set her cheeks on fire.

She crossed the few feet separating them and stuck out her hand. "Nice to see you again. I hear from Giovanni you may need some help updating security over at the Rio?"

"Bad news travels fast," said Vincent, his gaze penetrating. "Now that you're back I hope we can have an… intimate discussion about my problems."

"Oh, Vincent. I bet you say that to all the girls."

"Just the brilliant ones," he joked back.

After the party, Giovanni, Carla and Vincent adjourned to an office above the casino. Vincent leaned back in a leather chair, while a waiter served coffee and liqueurs.

"In two months, we have over 3000 women coming to the Rio for the RT Booklovers Convention. They were in Texas last year, and the security at the hotel was quite lax. A few rooms were robbed, including the owner's. She was *not* pleased." He motioned to the waiter for a refill. "We would like to start a long-term relationship with them since they're such a nice group, run up $5,000 a day in bar bills and party hearty. But that's not all, Hillary Clinton may be making an appearance at the convention. That means Secret Service. And I *know* DHS is involved in that."

"That means credit cards, jewelry, and merchandise from the convention can be stolen, not to mention possible protesters and security risks to the candidate. Purse checks and metal detectors will have to be brought in… you *do* have your hands full."

Giovanni stood up and stifled a yawn. "Late night for me. Good night, niece, and…" he lowered his voice into a conspiratorial whisper. "Don't do anything I wouldn't do." He gestured toward Vincent, who held open the door.

"Crime before love, uncle, crime before love," she replied. "Anyway, it's past my bedtime too."

Vincent's smile faded. Apparently, he'd been planning something. She let him walk her back to her suite, and they discussed plans to meet tomorrow. Before saying goodnight, she gave him a chaste kiss. Shutting the door, she let out a pent-up sigh. She still had work to do.

When Vincent was out of earshot, she made a call. "I'll be in your room in five minutes, you better be dressed and alone." Carla disconnected before Matt could respond. She had used her resort system log-in to look up the room number of his usual alias. It was too easy; he was lucky she wasn't a baddie.

This wasn't Budapest or Rome, where they had been forced to work under deep cover for weeks at a time, but Vegas. A leisurely roll in the hay was permissible here. After all, what happens in Vegas stays in Vegas. Mostly. Before they could start anything, she filled him in on the problems at the Rio. Like she had told her uncle, crime before love.

"Interesting. HQ got word that a cyberattack is imminent, they told me to pass it on to you. Word is, it's going to happen the weekend of April 17th."

"That's the same time as the convention and the candidate event."

"The department has an assignment for you. They want you to attend the convention—blend in with the writers and readers."

"Do they now. Looking for what? I'm curious."

His answer was lost to her. Matt had walked behind her and slowly unzipped her dress inch-by-inch before finally unhooking her bra. She let out a low moan.

"I'm supposed to be a romance author?" she asked over her shoulder. "I guess I could write about you. But I forgot the handcuffs and the leather belt."

"I didn't," he said. As he slowly undressed in front of her, whipping off his belt. "But I think that's considered erotica."

He turned off the light and tossed her on the bed.

***

The following day, after spending the morning in the tech support room checking on the computer gurus, Carla heeded the call of the all-powerful massage chair in her suite. Heels off and half asleep, she nearly jumped out of her skin when her phone rang.

"Lightfoot," Carla answered.

"Carla, it's Vincent. Can we meet for dinner?" He sounded worried, and she could hear the binging of an onslaught of messages in the background.

Maintaining security these days wasn't easy, but when your facility is at the top of the list of potential targets, *whammo*, instant heart attack. Years ago, it was all card counting, safe cracking and money laundering. Now it was stolen identities, credit card fraud and e-fencing—plus money laundering.

"Tell me something interesting, and maybe I'll consider it." Leaning back in the chair with a vibrating foot rest, all Carla wanted to do was relax.

He paused for a moment. His voice deepened, "You have such a lovely face. And lips, I remember your lips, Carla. I want my fingers…"

"Stick to business," she admonished. She remembered his lips too. "Seven-thirty in our bistro."

***

Matt was working at the restaurant bar and brought over wine glasses and a few extra cocktail napkins to the table. Carla noticed his chicken scratch on her napkin and switched it with a clean one as Matt uncorked the wine. She glanced at it under the table, it read: "Need to talk. Orders from above." She balled it up and tossed it in her purse.

The food was exquisite, and the wine well paired. Carla complimented Vincent on his choice. After dessert was cleared, she brought out her notebook and began to jot things down.

Their plans required doubling efforts to ensure all the upgrades were complete in time for the convention and hiring off-duty police in plainclothes. A manual of travel tips would be sent to all attendees, to make them aware and proactive in avoiding credit card fraud and thefts. Basic things like don't bring a debit card; a DO NOT DISTURB sign does not stop thieves; take valuables with you or put in them in the safe; lock your suitcase; notify your bank that you are going out of town; check your charges online, be wary using credit cards in gift shops and restaurants.

Carla thought it would be best to route Hillary into the ballroom via the kitchen. After readers and writers stream out, it would be time to bring in the union members who voted for her in the primary. Everyone would be forced to go through metal detectors set up at the entrance to the conference area.

All told, another fifty people needed to be hired.

At the end of the meal, Carla stretched, arching her back. The motion was intended to draw Matt's attention. She opened her fingers to indicate she needed ten minutes before he followed. Looking back,

Carla found Vincent's eyes glued to the front of her dress. She cleared her throat. He shrugged and flashed his devil-may-care smile.

On the boy, the smile was enough to make her weak-kneed. On the man, it was devastating. She readied her chant of "crime before love", but didn't get a chance to say it before he received a text and reluctantly stood up to leave.

"Thank you for a most pleasant evening. I'm sorry to say I have to put out some fires at the Rio. Let's talk again tomorrow." He placed a kiss on her palm, and left. It was her turn to be slack-jawed.

When she recovered, she shot Matt a text message: "Supply closet." A very unlikely place to be bugged. It suddenly hit her, that she'd never considered sweeping the Excelsior for bugs.

She turned the doorknob, and screamed as a hand grabbed her wrist and pulled her inside.

"You scared the crap out of me."

Matt rolled his eyes. "You've been distracted all night."

"It's just family business, none of your concern. Spill the beans or I kill the messenger."

He held up his hands in surrender. "DHS is officially putting you back in the game. They want you on the ground at the convention in a more visible position than the usual plainclothes." He shrugged. "Good news is, I found someone to help with your cover. There are hundreds of authors, but only a few female cover models. We have the perfect escort for you. You'll be demonstrating how to pose for a romance book cover."

She stared at him as the silence stretched on. "Are you going to tell me who it is?"

"Fabio," he blurted.

"Did you say… Fabio? As on the bodice ripper covers and 'I Can't Believe It's Not Butter', Fabio?"

He nodded. "The photographer will be one of our men."

The plan finally dawned on her. "No way! I'm not a model. I don't know how to pose. This is crazy! Where do I hide my gun, in his codpiece?"

"The upper levels had me approach Fabio, it wasn't my choice. Face it, you're a cover model now, Boss." He grinned.

***

That week, reports of hotel heists at the Mandalay Bay and the New York-New York were being investigated. All with the same MO—an increase in credit card fraud and identity theft, followed by cracked safes and rifled luggage in high profile client rooms.

The morning before the RT Booklovers Convention, Carla needed a break and decided to stroll around the hotel gardens. As she walked through the lobby of the Excelsior, reception was quiet, except for two attendants. A gorgeous new flower arrangement was positioned by the concierge sign. Alexander Braillowski was not at the desk, but she decided to take advantage of the quiet and, quite literally, smell the roses. The fragrance was faint, but divine. She sniffed again, and felt something bump her nose. She jumped back. Cautiously, she peered at the bloom. Seeing nothing, she removed the rose and shook it.

Something small and metallic fell onto the marble floor. Carla knelt down and examined the thin black disk for a moment before hurrying to shut down all the computers and peripherals. Pulling out the wireless detector from her purse, she switched it on. Sure enough, the tiny disk emitted a signal. She swept the concierge desk and found a bug on the bottom of Mr. Braillowski's nameplate.

She texted Vincent before continuing her sweep of the lobby. It revealed several more, black disks. She noted their locations but did not remove them. She wasn't ready to tip her hand to whoever was behind this.

Vincent met her in the tech room of the Excelsior. She put a finger over her lips as they walked in to make sure no one would give them away. She swept that room too, and found a hard drive, storing data from the bugged flowers. Meanwhile, Vincent's face was turning unattractive colors.

"Hey, Vincent, that program's almost finished. Let's go grab a bite to eat."

He nodded.

In the lobby they had a hurried discussion. "We've got to work fast, and we don't even know who's behind this."

"Don't you think it's obvious?" Vincent fumed. "It's your own people. And probably mine too."

"I'm not so sure. That hard drive could have been put there by anyone. The door wasn't even locked, and the tech guys know there are people coming in and out all day. We need an automatic lock with key pad placed on our doors immediately."

"Isn't that a bit like locking the barn door after the horses have escaped?"

But she knew the black disks could only account for part of the setup. *Who was listening, and how were they conducting the attacks?*

"We're running out of time."

***

Her worst nightmare had come true. Carla was freezing in a wispy gypsy skirt and revealing lace bodice. The photographer's lights were not nearly hot enough to chase away the chill. The only thing keeping her from hypothermia was the body heat of her partner who was embracing her tightly and gazing deeply into her eyes as hundreds of cameras flashed. Of course, *he* got to wear pants, tight-fitting though they were.

Fabio had been great, so supportive and helpful in making her look like a professional model. Next to someone who looked that good, there wasn't a whole lot for her to do. The DHS was right—the stage was the ideal place to scan for suspicious activity. She was sure every female in a five-mile radius had passed through this convention hall. At last count, the DHS had thirty scanners or more zapping the crowd. One fake gun, and three pairs of knitting needles, had already been found by the Secret Service.

Since every attendee had a smartphone, tablet or laptop of some sort, how was she supposed to find a hacker, let alone see past the crowd surrounding the authors signing?

While she was concentrating on holding still in a particularly ridiculous pose, Fabio repositioned her ear near his mouth, and whispered, "I think I see something strange."

"What?" Carla whispered back.

"A pack of women with rolling luggage. Not the book bags everyone else is carrying. Now they're regrouping, before they were acting like they didn't know each other. I'll lift you so you can see."

A moment later, Carla's head was above the crowd, and she saw the group he described.

"We need a break."

Fabio raised his voice. "We're taking fifteen."

A chorus of disappointed groans went up from the crowd as Fabio set Carla on the floor. She wrapped herself in a robe and spoke into her hidden mic.

"Do you have eyes on five women leaving the conference center dragging heavy wheeled bags?" She described their nearly identical striped luggage.

"Eyes on," Matt confirmed. "Do you want them taken into custody?"

"No, observe and report." At the hall doors, she went one way and Fabio went the other to divert the fans. Soon, she had a visual of the undercovers and the women. Those bags were too heavy to contain just a few signed books. She contacted Vincent at his post in tech tower.

"What are our infested flowers telling us?"

"A man is telling someone to move faster. He's parking his van and leaving in ten. Guess that explains how they're transporting the goods. We're monitoring data usage through the wi-fi repeaters, and haven't noted any significant surges yet."

"Grid eight," Vincent's voice interrupted across her transceiver.

"Matt, get some men to the loading dock."

Lucky number eight. Carla hotfooted it to the location. Readers with tote bags full of signed books jumped out of the way of the crazy woman in the robe. When she got to the dock, Carla didn't see either of the two people she expected. But looking at the van, everything fell into place. She took out her phone and dialed a number.

"Vegas Strip Florist, this is Natalie speaking. How may I help you?"

Bingo, thought Carla as she tracked the call and made her way toward the woman speaking. "Oh, hey, Natalie, this is Carla. About that date to catch up… I think I'll finally have the time." She pulled the phone away from her ear to relay the description and location to the team—in front of the metal detectors just inside the conference center entrance.

Natalie Logan saw Carla and lunged, moments before DHS reached them. Matt tackled her, and Natalie bit him. "You owe me," he said to Carla with a lascivious grin as he handcuffed the florist.

"You! You always have to win. You always have to be the best. It's all your fault." Natalie shrieked as she was being taken away. "This round isn't over yet! Be ready for some big surprises."

Fabio made his way through the police line, keeping back the crowd, and appeared beside Carla. "Dinner?" He interrupted smoothly. Carla smiled gratefully, tightening the sash of her robe.

"I'm not really dressed to go out, but I have a lovely suite and we can order in." She batted her eyelashes, took his arm and they posed for the camera. This time for real.

Vincent and Uncle Giovanni were trying to disperse the crowd and the news cameras. Hillary would be arriving soon. Carla nodded at the Secret Service agents monitoring the doorway.

"This has been an exhausting day, Fabio. I think we deserve champagne."

"At the very least," he whispered in her ear.

13Thirty Books

Exciting Thrillers, Heart-Warming Romance,
Mind-Bending Horror, Sci-Fantasy
and
Educational Non-Fiction

The Third Hour

The Third Hour is an original spin on the religious-thriller genre, incorporating elements of science fiction along with the religious angle. Its strength lies in this originality, combined with an interesting take on real historical figures, who are made a part of the experiment at the heart of the novel, and the fast pace that builds.

Ripper – A Love Story

"Queen Victoria would not be amused--but you will be by this beguiling combination of romance and murder. Is the Crown Prince of England really Jack the Ripper? His wife would certainly like to know... and so will you."
Diana Gabaldon, New York Times Best Selling Author

Heather Graham's Haunted Treasures

Presented together for the first time, New York Times Bestselling Author, Heather Graham brings back three tales of paranormal love and adventure.

Heather Graham's Christmas Treasures

New York Times Bestselling Author, Heather Graham brings back three out-of-print Christmas classics that are sure to inspire, amaze, and warm your heart.

Zodiac Lovers Series

Zodiac Lovers is a series of romantic, gay, paranormal novelettes. In each story, one of the lovers has all the traits of his respective zodiacal sign.

Never Fear

Shh... Something's Coming

Never Fear – Phobias

Everyone Fears Something

Never Fear – Christmas Terrors

He sees you when you're sleeping ...

And more in the Never Fear Series

Stop Saying Yes – Negotiate!

Stop Saying Yes - Negotiate! is the perfect "on the go" guide for all negotiations. This easy-to-read, practical guide will enable you to quickly identify the other side's tactics and strategies allowing you to defend yourself ensuring a better negotiation for your side and theirs.